"I *hate wanting you.*"

Kane continued, "I hate looking at you and knowing that you're not only the one woman I ache to have, but the last one I want."

Heartache took the last of Rio's strength. She let her hands slide from Kane's wide shoulders and her arms fall onto the bed. She all but wilted beneath the warm crush of his hard body, her face turned away, tears leaking from her eyes.

"I hate wanting you, too, Kane," she whispered. "I'm ashamed that I've loved someone all these years who holds me in such contempt...."

Dear Reader,

Welcome to the next book in our exciting showcase for 1997!
Once again we're delighted to bring you a specially chosen
story we know you're going to enjoy again and again....

Authors you'll treasure, books you'll want to keep!

This month's recommended reading is *Wild at Heart* by
Susan Fox, a romance full of emotion and intensity that will
leave you breathless! Susan is a lifelong fan of Westerns
and cowboys, and tends to think of heroes in terms of
Stetsons and boots!

Susan Fox loves to hear from readers! You can write to her
at: P.O. Box 35681, Des Moines, Iowa 50315, U.S.A.

Books by Susan Fox

HARLEQUIN ROMANCE
2930—THE BLACK SHEEP
2983—NOT PART OF THE BARGAIN
3268—THE BAD PENNY
3432—THE COWBOY WANTS A WIFE!

Don't miss any of our special offers. Write to us at the
following address for information on our newest releases.

Harlequin Reader Service
U.S.: 3010 Walden Ave., P.O. Box 1325, Buffalo, NY 14269
Canadian: P.O. Box 609, Fort Erie, Ont. L2A 5X3

Wild at Heart
Susan Fox

Harlequin Books

TORONTO • NEW YORK • LONDON
AMSTERDAM • PARIS • SYDNEY • HAMBURG
STOCKHOLM • ATHENS • TOKYO • MILAN
MADRID • WARSAW • BUDAPEST • AUCKLAND

ISBN 0-373-03468-7

WILD AT HEART

First North American Publication 1997.

Copyright © 1997 by Susan Fox.

CHAPTER ONE

"I HEAR B. J. Hastings proposed."

Kane Langtry's voice carried a sarcasm that made Rio stiffen. She glanced his way briefly in the dim stable, then returned her attention to the glossy red hide of the sorrel she was brushing. The secret shame she'd lived with for as long as she could remember welled up. She knew precisely why B.J. wanted to marry her, and his reasons had nothing to do with love or respect—or even the desire he pretended.

It hurt that Kane had decided to corner her on the subject. She knew immediately that he meant to hammer it all home to her as if she were too infatuated with the neighboring rancher to see it for herself.

Her softly challenging, "So?" was much less defiant than she'd meant and she instantly regretted it.

"So, I sure as hell hope you know that B.J. and his daddy see you as a way out of their money troubles."

The low words cut cruelly. The subtle reminder that she was unworthy of being one of Sam Langtry's heirs was another cut.

Rio finished with the sorrel and tossed the brush to a nearby hay bale. She gave Kane a lazy smile to cover her hurt. "You don't think hot sex had anything to do with it, huh?"

Kane's expression grew hard and his eyes wandered down her slim, feminine figure. It was a critical inspection, insolent, lingering and ultimately derisive before his gaze came back up to hers. "If you've been giving it out, then it's even more certain Langtry money is his only reason for proposing marriage."

Kane's animosity toward her was as relentless as it was heartbreaking, but Rio kept her smile in place as she looked up into his harsh features. "Jealous, Kane?" The question was retaliation for his cruel remarks. Rio knew—she'd always known—that Kane considered her little more than white trash. The suggestion that he desired her in any way was exactly the slap she meant it to be.

The arrogant lines of his handsome face became more pronounced and the dark glitter in his blue eyes was cold as he took a step closer. His voice was quiet, its silky tone all the more dangerous because it was so controlled.

"I could have you anytime I decided to, Rio." His hand came up and he caught a wisp of dark hair that had worked loose from her braid. A gentle tug sent an avalanche of sensation through her that made her breath catch. A second later, she realized by the faint twist of his mouth that her shock—and her helpless reaction to his touch—had exposed the hungry longing for him that she'd labored to keep hidden.

Rio had loved Kane Langtry for years. Not for his harshness or indifference toward her, but for the man he was with everyone else. In spite of his refusal to accept her into his family, Rio admired him. She'd looked up to him first as a foster brother, but had rapidly developed a crush on him that had nothing to do with sisterly feelings. By the time she'd turned eighteen, she'd come to the unhappy realization that she was in love with a man who saw her ongoing presence in his life as an irritation.

But irritation wasn't the impression she got in those charged moments as she stared up into his face. There was a fierceness about him now, though his fingers still toyed gently with the wisp of hair. The dark sensuality that suddenly burned in his gaze was so intense that she was seized by a strange paralysis. Her knees went weak and she could barely breathe as the back of his finger grazed the side of her throat. The husky timbre of his voice was hypnotic.

"Tell him no, Rio. Not even B.J. deserves a woman who's lovesick over another man."

It took a moment for Kane's blunt words to penetrate. It was that same moment that Kane lowered his head and his chiseled lips came to within a finger space of her parted ones. His hand slipped around the back of her neck to hold her in place, but Rio was so astonished by Kane's sudden advance that she couldn't move. Kane had never, ever touched her like this. His last-second hesitation merely heightened the sensual confusion that whirled over her.

And then his mouth crashed forcefully against hers. The twisting pressure of his lips opened hers and she gasped as she was crushed against his hard, lean body. The raw pleasure of his lips was devastating, and Rio clung to him, unable to withstand the sensual onslaught.

Kane Langtry had been the subject of every wild dream she'd ever had, however foolish, however futile. But she'd never dreamed this, never suspected that any man anywhere was capable of bestowing such pleasure or demanding such an uninhibited response. Rio had never imagined she could lose control of herself, never pictured recovering from her initial shock and returning his kiss with the fervor she did.

But she was wrapped around him, her long fingers combed tightly into his thick, dark hair as she met and returned what his mouth was doing to hers. Reduced to impulse and instinct, she was slow to realize that Kane ultimately controlled the passion he'd forced upon her. He withdrew from her in measured stages, and Rio couldn't help her whimper of disappointment when his kiss began to ease.

By the time his lips finally moved off hers, her legs could barely support her weight. The few kisses she'd had in the past were nothing like the rough mating Kane had given her. It was horrifying that he'd so thoroughly disoriented her and that she'd been so quickly driven to such abandon. Arousal still throbbed heavily through her and she was alarmed to discover that she was powerless against it.

It was her powerlessness that made Kane's iron-willed control all the more awful for her. She opened her eyes and looked up into his hard features, stricken by the faint twist at one corner of the mouth that had so completely mastered hers.

"Tell him no, Rio," he rasped, the roughness of

his voice making it sound harsh and condemning to her. "B.J. would want to have a wife that's all his."

Rio swayed when Kane abruptly released her and stepped back to retrieve his Stetson. She hated that she had to put out a hand to the stall door to steady herself. Kane watched her intently, his eyes burning with new knowledge. Whatever he'd suspected before about her feelings, there were no mysteries now.

Rio was left with nothing to hide behind. Her usual cool indifference, mild defiance—even the sham of allowing B.J. Hastings to date her, would no longer convince anyone but outsiders that she didn't have feelings for Kane Langtry.

Kane had stripped her of everything in the past few moments. The fact that she'd helped him do it was something she wouldn't get over for a very long time.

There was something edgy and restless about Rio Cory when she came up to the main house late that afternoon. Sam Langtry noticed it the moment she stepped into the kitchen from the back door and tugged off her Stetson to hang it on a wall peg. She hadn't seen him yet, sitting at the table in the breakfast nook off to her right, so he had an opportunity to study her.

The eleven-year-old orphan he'd taken in had grown into a beauty. Her waist-length braid was nearly black, her dark-lashed eyes large and jewel blue, but her delicate features promised an enduring beauty that age would never diminish. Just like her mama.

In many ways, Rio reminded Sam Langtry of the woman he'd loved but had never married. The biggest heartache of his seventy years was the fact that Lenore Cory's frail health had given out two years before her drunken husband had got himself killed. While she'd been alive, Sam had hinted to no one that he'd been in love with her. He'd done everything propriety, and Lenore's pride, allowed to help her and her child. Later, he'd taken in her orphaned daughter after her husband's death. Raising Rio had been a balm for the loss of her mother.

But fourteen years after Lenore's death, Sam had come to the end of his time on the earth. His heart was failing, he could feel it weaken by the hour. It was now, when he made himself take stock of his life and his deeds, that his memories of the past had come so clear. He was surprised sometimes at the depth of his feelings, but it was a soul-deep pleasure that his memories of Lenore had grown even more precious to him.

As her daughter was precious to him. Sam loved his son, loved his stepdaughter, Tracy, but Rio shared equally in his love for the children he considered his. The fact that he felt more tender toward her than he did Kane or Tracy was because Rio had always been the one who'd needed him most. She'd been deprived of the most, had lost the most. She'd also given back the most with her love and unswerving loyalty to him.

His only regret in dying was that he knew Rio would take his death hard. For all she'd become, for all her strengths, she was still that lost, frightened child who ran wild after her mama died, then had run off to hide on Langtry range after her father was killed. The wounds that had been inflicted on her because of her father's drunkenness and the notoriety of the fatal accident he'd caused still undermined her confidence, still kept her from feeling fully the pride she should have had in being a vital part of Langtry.

Perhaps he should have legally adopted her after all. His hope for Rio and Kane to fall in love, marry and together carry on the impressive history of Langtry Ranch now seemed every bit the foolish romanticism of an old man. Kane and Rio had never seemed less likely to forge such a bond. Rio loved Kane deeply, though she'd carefully kept it to herself. Kane appeared to be indifferent to Rio—when he wasn't jumping down her throat about something. He'd never been more critical of her than lately, but then, Sam knew his taciturn son well enough to suspect that his criticisms might be an effort to make sure he kept Rio at a distance. After all, Rio was a beauty, as skilled and capable as either of them in the running of Langtry. And there was a powerful tension between the two of them. Sam hoped his plan would keep them together long enough after his death for the tension to be resolved.

Rio turned her head just then and saw him at the table. Her edginess vanished, and a smile came over her lips. Her feminine stride as she crossed the kitchen to lean down and kiss his cheek was loose and relaxed, but the moment her hand touched his shoulder, he felt the tremor in it.

"I hope that's decaf you're swillin', cowboy," she said, then stepped over to the counter to help herself to the coffeemaker that held the real thing.

"Decaf coffee, no red meat, no liquor, no cigars, no salt, no fat, no fun. If it weren't for sugar, I'd have no vices whatsoever," he grumbled with good humor.

Sam was watching Rio's face closely when she turned back. He noted the slight swelling of her lips before she took a sip of coffee. He hoped B.J. Hastings wasn't responsible for the telltale fullness.

Rio had told him about B.J.'s proposal. She'd also confided that she thought B.J. was really after a Langtry loan. Sam suspected B.J. was after the impressive inheritance he meant to bestow on her. That Rio had called B.J.'s sudden interest in marrying her a bid for a loan reflected her lack of presumption where inheritance was concerned. She'd made it clear to him the first time he'd brought up the subject of her share in his estate that she wanted to inherit nothing from him. He'd given her the most important things in her life, she'd declared, so she wouldn't need his money. The only thing she'd asked was that he put something in his will to compel Kane and his heirs to allow her to return to the ranch from time to time.

Rio's wishes where his will was concerned were worlds different than his second wife's. As if she'd forgotten their prenuptial agreement, Ramona had already gone over every bank balance, investment, stock portfolio and business holding, and had handed him a lengthy list of the ones she wanted for herself. Her wish list had been the most blatantly greedy demand she'd ever made of him. She didn't realize yet that he'd found out about her infidelities. But it was because of her secret mistreatment of Rio that he meant to see that Ramona didn't receive a nickel more than the law assigned a surviving wife. She had a legal right to half of everything he'd earned during their six year marriage, but because the law allowed it and because of the prenuptial agreement, that made Langtry Ranch and the lion's share of Langtry holdings and stocks exempt. Ramona was certain to pitch a world-class tantrum when she found out that he wasn't going to be generous, but Sam believed the purpose of a will was as much to reward or insult heirs as it was to divide the deceased's assets. The idea appealed to his sense of justice.

"You got time for a drive up to the Painted Fence?"

Sam's question sent a ripple of unease through Rio. She set her coffee aside to give herself time to recover. Sam referred to the family cemetery on Langtry as the Painted Fence. That he'd wanted to visit the small, private cemetery with increasing frequency the past few weeks was another reminder to Rio that he believed his life was near the end.

The thought was unbearable. Sam was not just the only real father she'd ever had, he was her dearest friend. It was inconceivable that the tall, strong man whose word was law on Langtry could actually die.

Her quiet, "Give me a moment to wash up," was all she could get out before she turned and forced herself to make a sedate exit from the kitchen. Rio managed a reserved smile for Ardis and Estelle, the cook and the housekeeper, as she passed them in the back hall, but the moment she reached the refuge of the small bath, she closed the door and leaned against it.

The anguish that had disrupted her sleep for weeks was suddenly agonizing. Sam was dying. He refused to consult another heart specialist and had warned both her and Kane that he wanted no heroic efforts to extend his life. That included the wheelchair Kane had bought, which had been banished to a garage. All Sam agreed to was his special diet, his medications and his naps. Rio was powerless to change his mind, powerless against the rapid advance of his illness.

Her mother's death had been long and slow. Rio had been just as powerless against it. In the end, it seemed her mother had just given up, first resisting ongoing treatments, then finally refusing them altogether. She'd died very soon after, leaving her only child to a neglectful, alcoholic father. Those had been black days, with no warmth, no affection in the little house they'd lived in on Langtry for as long as she could remember. By then, her father's drinking binges lasted for days, and Rio was so ashamed and afraid of him that she spent nearly all the time she wasn't in school working odd jobs around the ranch or exploring the land. More often than not, she slept in one of the barn lofts or hay barns, anything to avoid her father's rages and drunken stupors.

And yet, Ned Cory's death two years after her mother's had been anything but a relief. Because he'd caused the highway accident that had also killed two teenage brothers, the notoriety of his drinking had mushroomed, making Rio more an object of scorn than sympathy. His death had also cost her the last of what little she'd had: the right to live on Langtry and have some sort of home.

But she'd lived a long time on her own, keeping out of the way, doing what she could to keep herself fed, clothed and attending school. The social worker who'd showed up hadn't been convinced an eleven-year-old could do such things, and had insisted on placing her with a foster family in the city. The woman's overbearing manner gave Rio no confidence in any family the woman would choose for her, so she'd fled. She'd known all the best places to hide around the ranch headquarters, known several ideal places on the range. She hadn't been able to risk going back to the little house, except for a few things which she'd taken away and carefully hidden. She stopped going to school, too, afraid the social worker would have too much help from the principal and teachers. She'd finally got so hungry that she'd made nightly raids on the cook house, plundering the food store and enjoying the furnace heat for as long as she dared before she climbed back out a window into the chilly fall night.

Until Kane had caught her leaving one night with a pillowcase of food. Until he'd hauled her to the main house to face his father as the fugitive and thief she'd become.

Sam Langtry, as always, had seemed a giant of a

man—and never more so than on that night when he'd
looked down on the ragged, dusty child who'd stood
before him with her pillowcase of stolen food.

"Who owns what's under your feet, girl?" he'd
asked in that low, gravelly drawl. Though his tone
was soft, it carried the unmistakable authority of a
powerful man whose word on any subject was final.

Rio's quiet "You do, sir," was wary. After eleven
years of living with a father who yelled and smashed
things with his big fists over every minor irritation,
she'd been prepared to vault out of harm's way at the
smallest sign of anger from Sam Langtry.

"Do you figure I got some say around here?" he'd
asked her next, all the while staring so steadily and
deeply into her eyes that Rio felt he could see everything bad and wrong in her.

"You're the boss," she'd got out, and realized
sickly that no matter how hard she'd tried not to be
taken away, no matter how much she feared having
to go with the social worker, she would. She'd have
to if Sam Langtry decreed it, and she'd mind him fast
and with no complaint because she was terrified of
him.

"If you know that, how come you didn't think to
come talk to me?" It had been a stunning question.
Rio never would have risked actually facing this man
for any reason for a talk. He'd been nice to her in the
past, but her mother had been around then. The foreman let her do odd jobs for money, but for almost
two years she'd done her best to stay out of Sam
Langtry's sight. Her father had always been in trouble

and Rio was ashamed of that. Besides, no one seemed to like her any better than they had her father. Now, she was completely on her own. She had nothing, she was nothing. Trash like her didn't dare pester anyone, especially someone as important as Sam Langtry.

"Are you shy?" The hard line of Sam's mouth bent a little with the question, but his look was just as direct, just as penetrating.

"I'm scared." The horrifying admission slipped out and Rio felt her face go hot.

"No need to be scared, girl," he said, then asked, "How about somethin' hot to eat, an' maybe a piece of apple pie to top it off?"

The question caught her off guard. Her nervous gaze veered toward the big clock over the door behind the big rancher. "But it's the middle of the night," she said, then caught her breath, suddenly worried that he'd think she was arguing with him.

"Might be, but a meal sounds good." He stepped away from her to the hall from the big kitchen to call out, "Hey, Ardis! If you're up, we could use somethin' hot to eat out here."

To Rio's astonishment, the cook had shuffled into the kitchen in a robe and fuzzy slippers, her dark hair wound over brushy rollers. Her eyebrows climbed high when she saw Rio, but her mouth was a noncommittal line.

"Is this that Cory girl?"

The cook's blunt question embarrassed Rio. She heard herself referred to that way often, and never in a kind way.

"This is Miz Lenore's daughter, Rio," Sam said, his choice of words somehow a correction. "While we were talkin', I got hungry for an early breakfast—steak, eggs, toast and some of them spicy potato chunks. Hot chocolate, if we got some, Ardis. And apple pie. Miz Rio's gonna join me, so you'd better make plenty."

Ardis's brisk "hmm" as she looked over Rio's dusty clothes was disapproving, but she moved off toward the refrigerator to get started.

That night marked the biggest turning point of Rio's young life. It had been more stunning than the death of either of her parents, more unexpected than anything in her eleven years and, because of Sam's kindness, more wonderful than anything a lonely, frightened child could have ever dared hope.

And now the man who'd done that for her, the man who'd taken her in, treated her like his own and given her more love and understanding and stability than she'd ever known, was dying.

The reminder hurt, the daily evidence of his decline filled her with despair. Her life wouldn't be the same without him. She could bear the loss of Langtry, she could bear having to leave and lose her last hope that Kane would ever truly accept her. She couldn't bear to lose Sam.

Rio quickly turned on the cold water tap and splashed her face with water. She resolved then to stay close to the house, close to Sam. There weren't many days left, and certainly not many days until Ramona and Tracy were due home for a short respite from the social whirl of Dallas. Until then, she would spend all the time with Sam that she could. She'd do her best to cater to every whim he had. And if that included a hundred trips to the Painted Fence, she'd make certain she took him on every one.

Sam got his hat and ambled out the back door. The heat from the late-afternoon sun was overpowering now that his heart was so susceptible to the stress of temperature extremes. The big ranch pickup he and Rio normally used for their little excursions had a good air conditioner, so he made his way around the pool and across the huge back patio toward where they'd left it the day before.

His chest hurt and he was out of breath by the time he reached the truck and climbed into the passenger side. He leaned over and twisted the key that had been left in the ignition. It didn't take long before the cool air from the compressor rushed through the vents at him, but it took a little longer to get his breath back and for the ache in his chest to ease.

By then, Kane was walking up the lane from one of the stables. He changed direction when he saw his father in the idling pickup.

"Where's Rio?" The stern line of his son's mouth implied that Rio was remiss for not being close by.

Sam leaned his arm on the bottom of the open truck window and watched his son's expression closely. "She'll be along in a minute. Has B.J. been around today?"

The mention of B. J. Hastings made Kane's frown

deepen and Sam was relieved to see it. Kane's terse, "No. Why?" was the opportunity Sam had hoped for.

"Rio came in a while ago, lookin' like someone had kissed the daylights outta her." Sam leveled his gaze on his son's hard expression, then felt a run of satisfaction when Kane didn't remark.

"Whoever it was, oughta take it easy. Rio's worked awful hard around here to earn the men's respect. Wouldn't do for someone to jeopardize that."

Kane's hard expression went black. "Rio can be responsible for her own reputation."

Sam wasn't at all intimidated by his son. "That's right, but Rio's more vulnerable than most to gossip."

"Then she should hurry up and marry B.J., or cut the poor sucker loose."

"Rio's had a lot to live down. She's careful about who she offends. Cuttin' B.J. loose will take some unhurried finesse and a lot of diplomacy. You and I might soften the blow by scraping up a loan to help the Hastings out."

Kane swore. "B.J. is a world-class spendthrift. All a loan's gonna do is give him another few turns around the drain."

"Yeah, he and his daddy would rather get their hands on a meal ticket than a loan anyway, which explains the marriage proposal. Neither one of them sees a value in Rio beyond dollar signs."

Kane's mouth tightened and he glanced away from his father. "Hell, Rio could be in love with him."

Sam gave a hoarse chuckle. "B.J. is too much his daddy's little boy to appeal to Rio. Besides, any man who takes a shine to that girl is already being measured against an impossible standard.''

Kane didn't comment directly, but gave an irritable grunt. His father wasn't finished with the subject, however.

"And just in case you didn't take my meaning earlier, Mr. Impossible Standard, you go easy on that girl.''

Kane's gaze swung back to his father's and narrowed. He'd assumed Sam was the impossible standard Rio measured other men against. On the other hand, he should have realized his father would never have used such words to describe himself. It would have been conceited. But to hear Sam bluntly remind him of his status as the object of Rio's hero worship angered him. "Rio needs to grow out of her adolescent crush.''

Sam tipped his head back slightly to study him for a long moment. "Then don't play kissing games with her, Kane. She doesn't have your experience, and she'll never be as hard bit. You could hurt somethin' real special in her.''

Kane felt his anger mount. Rio Cory was as tempting to him as she was an irritant. He wasn't certain anymore that there was any real difference between the two feelings. It was bad enough that at twenty-three she still lived on Langtry Ranch. The eleven-year-old orphan he'd caught stealing food from the cook house had grown into a Texas beauty. Despite the fact that she worked on Langtry as hard as any ranch hand, there was a polish to her now, a feminine allure he wouldn't have imagined from someone with her background. And yet, there was something not quite tame about her, a wariness that made him think of a green-broke mustang more accustomed to following its wild instincts than submitting to a firm hand on the reins.

His father had gained her trust, her loyalty and her love. But then, Sam had taken her in, given her a home and provided her with the chance to be something more than she would have been had her father lived. In return, Rio idolized his father, devoted herself to him like a daughter and lived up to his expectations. It was no secret to Kane that Sam fancied Rio a suitable marriage choice for his only son.

And that made Rio Cory the subject of the only real argument between father and son. Their other disputes were centered largely in the realm of business. Rio was the lightning rod of their personal disagreements. Kane had opposed Sam's decision to take in the scrawny little thief. She'd had a rough childhood, had run wild for years and the Cory name had made her an outcast in their ranching community. Besides, Kane had known that she was a reminder to his father of things best forgotten. Despite Kane's objections, Sam was almost obsessed on the subject of protecting Rio and compensating her for her dismal childhood. To her credit, she'd rarely allowed Sam to give her much besides food, shelter and basic clothing. She'd worked on Langtry for ranch hand's wages since high school and had been smart enough to win scholarships to put herself through college.

She'd soaked up every bit of the affection and attention Sam had offered, and the bond between the two was unshakable. Nevertheless, Kane didn't want to be Rio's reward or Sam's replacement when he died, so his father's subtle maneuverings to put Rio in his path was something he felt compelled to resist.

His terse, "Then warn her off," was heartfelt.

Sam gave his son a narrow look. "Are you tellin' me Rio's been throwin' herself at you?" The slant that came to his mouth showed his skepticism.

Kane growled a curse and his dark gaze flicked away. "A female doesn't have to throw herself at a man to send the signal that she's his for the taking."

"A lot of red-blooded Texas men would give ten years off their lives if Rio would send them that signal," Sam declared, the pride in his voice bringing his son's angry gaze back to his.

"Then she should pick one of them."

Sam shook his head and gazed out the windshield of the idling pickup to focus into the distance. "Rio lives by her instincts. She's like a wild mustang filly who's drawn to the biggest, toughest stallion. She's got to survive the elements and the predators. She's too savvy to bother with a weaker, less decisive male. She needs one who's strong enough to take on whatever comes along and survive the longest. She's already lost a lot. When I die, she'll lose again. She'll be lookin' for someone durable."

Kane chuckled harshly at the mustang analogy that so closely matched his own perceptions of Rio, but there was no amusement in his tone. "You're gettin' whimsical in your old age, Daddy."

"Closer I get to the end, the simpler and more clear it's all becoming. Most things between a man and a woman aren't complicated, once they have some care for what each of them needs." Sam turned his head and looked at his implacable son. "Rio wouldn't be such a touchy subject if you'd pay more attention to your own instincts and followed them awhile."

One corner of Kane's mouth quirked. "Followed an instinct today...qualified for this lecture." With that, Kane took a step away from the pickup and nodded his head in the direction of the back patio. "The wild child's comin' this way. Don't get yourself tired out."

Rio didn't let her stride falter when she saw Kane standing beside the pickup. She felt heat rush to her face, then endured the inevitable disappointment and relief when Kane turned away and walked off toward the stable. Her heart sank a little when she saw the grim line of his mouth. She could always tell when Kane and his father were having a disagreement. That she was usually the cause made her heart sink a bit more.

Soon, there wouldn't be any more disagreements. The dismal reminder was suddenly oppressive.

CHAPTER TWO

Rio managed to get through the first few minutes at supper that night by simply not looking Kane's way. It was difficult to do, since he sat across from her. She felt more awkward with him than ever after that torrid kiss in the stable, and wished with all her heart she'd had the good sense to shove him away. Of all the things she'd had to live down, living down her wild response to Kane was made worse by the fact that this was one embarrassment she'd earned all by herself. It helped that he would never tell anyone else about it. It was certain she never would. But the knowledge that Kane was usually unforgiving toward her made the notion of redeeming herself in his eyes a near impossibility.

It was Sam who broke the uneasy silence at the table. "Aren't we gettin' that new bull tomorrow?"

"He's due by nine, but Rio may have to take delivery," Kane answered. "I've got an eight-thirty phone call. If I'm not finished by the time the truck gets here, she can see to it."

Rio accepted the indirect order from Kane as a matter of course. Since Sam's retirement, Kane was the boss. Rio was in charge when Kane was away or unavailable. The foreman took his orders from her in those instances, but she'd learned long ago that he and the ranch hands were competent enough not to need a taskmaster to map out their day. The men deferred to her because Sam's regard for her had ensured it. Rio showed her respect for their experience and competence by issuing few directives. The delivery of the expensive bull required one of them be present to accept it, but because Kane had spent a veritable fortune on the animal, Rio hoped this particular responsibility wouldn't fall to her.

She knew better than to let Kane know how she felt about it, however. Kane tolerated her position in the chain of command because of his father and because she'd managed to never give him an excuse to exclude her. Rio never trifled with Kane's orders and instructions. She'd just have to be especially vigilant to be certain the bull arrived in fit condition and that he was unloaded and settled in with special care.

It was Kane who brought up the next subject. "Ramona called while the two of you were out. She and Tracy will be here by tomorrow afternoon."

Though the news wasn't unexpected, Rio couldn't help the disappointment she felt. Or the tension. Ramona delighted in her petty torments, particularly since she'd learned early on that Rio never reported them to Sam.

Sam's only remark was, "It's about time." Rio didn't remark at all. She knew Sam wasn't happy that Ramona's idea of being a rancher's wife was to live most of the year at her penthouse in Dallas spending Langtry money. Rio usually made herself scarce when Ramona came home, both to avoid the woman and to ensure that Sam had as much time with his wife and stepdaughter as possible. She wouldn't this time, however. Because of Sam's health, Rio meant to remain close to the house.

"I need you to help me with paperwork tonight."

Kane's statement brought her gaze up to meet his briefly before she forced herself to look away. She dared a quiet, "Is this something new?" Kane took care of the lion's share of paperwork, just as he wanted. Rio had barely touched anything to do with papers or book work since Sam had retired. She suspected Kane's mention of paperwork was a ruse in order to speak to her alone, but she still felt shaken by what had happened in the stable that day.

"Come see for yourself."

Rio couldn't help another swift glance at Kane. She'd heard distinctly the challenge in his tone, but nothing on his harsh features confirmed her impression until he reached for his coffee cup and leaned back in his chair. His eyes met hers with a suddenness that sent a tiny shock through her system. The slow lift of one corner of his mouth was pure male arrogance and she felt her cheeks burn. Somehow she managed to keep her gaze steady with his until he broke contact and finished his coffee.

Kane soon excused himself and went off to the den. Rio and Sam headed off to the informal family room at the back of the big ranch house. After a leisurely game of checkers, Sam went to his room for the night. Though he told Rio he planned to watch a movie video before he went to sleep, she secretly doubted

he would. He seemed unusually tired tonight, and she
was grateful for the small elevator Kane had installed
in a storage closet off the back hall. Sam had refused
to have his bedroom moved down to the main floor
when his doctors had restricted him from using the
stairs. When he'd returned home from a hospital stay
to find an elevator in operation, he'd taken severe ex-
ception. He'd used it grudgingly, but three months
ago, he'd stopped disparaging it.

And that was another measure of his declining
health, she was reminded, and felt the familiar melancholy descend. A long walk, or better, an evening
horseback ride might have lifted her spirits a bit and
made it easier to sleep, but she doubted either choice
would work any better tonight than they had all the
other nights she'd tried them. Besides, Kane expected
her to join him and she'd avoided his summons as
long as she dared.

Rio made her way to the den, her nerves stretching
tight as she was forced to face Kane privately. Why
had he kissed her, why had he even touched her?
Since it would never happen again, she'd rather not
have known precisely what it was like to be in his
arms at the mercy of what his mouth could do to hers.
And she'd handed him a very painful means to torment her, if he chose. Because of that torrid kiss, she
no longer had any secrets from Kane that mattered.

She slowed her step as she reached the den, then
knocked softly on the open door before she walked
in. Kane sat at his desk, shuffling through a stack of

invoices. He didn't look up, didn't offer any pleas-
antry, but got straight to the point.

"After the bull's delivered in the morning, you can
make the circuit of line shacks and cow camps. Take
a cell phone and enough clothes to last you a few
days."

Rio stiffened. Normally, checking the line shacks
and cow camps for repairs and restocking their supplies was a days-long chore she might have welcomed
with Ramona coming home. Now that Sam was so ill,
she didn't intend to absent herself from the main
house for longer than a handful of hours at a time.

Telling Kane that, however, meant she'd be refusing an order. Her presence at the house for the dura-
tion of Ramona and Tracy's stay also meant increased
tension for them all, but for Kane in particular who
usually went out of his way to make their visit as
pleasant as possible.

Rio cleared her throat quietly, aware that Kane had
yet to look up and that his ongoing perusal of invoices
meant she'd been dismissed. Her soft, "I can't do it
now," was met with as much surprise as she'd expected.

Kane stilled, his blue eyes rising to hers and going
hard. "Why not?"

"Sam's..." Rio hesitated, lifted one shoulder,
loathe to put anything pessimistic about Sam into
words. "He's a little frail right now. I want to stay
close."

Kane tossed the papers aside. "Did it ever occur to

you that Ramona might not want to have you hovering? She might want to have Sam to herself."

His criticism stung. But then, most things Kane said to her did. On the other hand, Ramona could seem to do no wrong where Kane was concerned. The years-long frustration of being a target of Kane's disapproval while he turned a blind eye to Ramona's persistent lack of interest in her husband or his health was suddenly sharp.

But Rio knew better than to breathe a word of criticism about Sam's wife. Her chin came up a fraction and her lips thinned into a cynical line. "Ramona can have Sam to herself as much as she likes. Besides, I haven't seen Tracy for a long time."

"And Ramona likes it that way," he stated with brutal candor.

Rio glanced away from his harsh expression, suddenly weary. Maybe she had stayed on Langtry years longer than she should have. It didn't seem to matter to anyone but Sam that she'd spent that time working hard, laboring to repay all his kindnesses. To everyone else, she was still an outsider, an intruder who'd lucked into a fine, rich home that she hadn't deserved.

Bitterness and pride brought her gaze back to meet Kane's as she quietly asserted, "As long as Sam's alive, no one's going to chase me off, Kane. You and Ramona should know that by now."

Kane leaned back in his chair, his blue gaze cutting over her. "I don't want Sam upset."

Rio nodded. "Be sure you tell Ramona the same."

From the flare of annoyance in Kane's eyes, she

knew he still considered her the only one responsible
for the friction between her and Ramona. Ramona had
never had to be particularly clever to achieve that impression, not when Kane was so willing to see Rio as
the antagonist.

The reminder sent Rio's spirits lower. Kane would
never see the witch beneath Ramona's startling beauty
and Southern belle facade. Just as he would never
credit Rio with being anything more than Ned Cory's
daughter.

She gave him a grim twist of lips that acknowledged the unhappy fact, then turned and left the room
with brittle dignity.

Rio whipped off her dark Stetson and ran the back of
her wrist sleeve across her damp forehead. She put
the hat back on and yanked it down snugly as she
watched the back end of the stock trailer roll toward
her again.

Her quick, "Slow it down, cowboy!" was loud
enough to be heard by the driver, as was her curt, "A
little to the left."

The driver of the supercab pickup towing the trailer
reacted just as insolently to her directions as he had
for the past five minutes. She bit back a swear word
as the trailer again went too far to the right to line up
with the narrow alley that would channel the bull toward the corral she had selected for him. That the
trailer was still moving too fast to stop until it
slammed into the far side fence post was just one

more aggravation on a hot Texas morning full of aggravations.

The hooves of the startled bull inside the trailer hit the door like a cannon volley. Incensed, Rio started for the driver's side door of the truck.

The wide, fleshy face with a half-burned cigar stuck in its thick lips grinned out at her with more than a hint of mockery. "Sorry there, boss lady. You aren't too good at givin' directions, are ya? Maybe one of yer men could do better."

The enraged bull inside the trailer was rocking both it and the pickup in his effort to break out. If he injured himself, there'd be hell to pay, and Kane would hold her responsible.

Rio reached up and yanked open the door. Her sudden move was enough to startle the grin off the cowboy's sweaty face. "Step out or move aside." She lifted a boot to the running board of the big pickup to indicate not only her preference but her hurry. "One or the other, cowboy, or you'll be hauling that bull back."

"Ain't no one but me drivin' this truck." The sweaty cowboy sounded more like a whiny child than a man.

Rio's brisk, "Suit yourself," and her step off the running board was punctuated by a tight, "Give Mr. Cameron my regards, and tell him Langtry Ranch regrets we couldn't take delivery."

"Now hold on—" the cowboy called out as Rio walked away. She stopped and looked back at him.

"Out or over." Her firm tone brought a petulant

frown to the fleshy face, but the cowboy bit down on his cigar and wallowed to the middle of the bench seat.

Rio was behind the wheel in an instant, taking a second to check the side mirrors before she slipped the truck into gear and started it forward a few feet. The bull was too stirred up now to waste another moment. As she stopped the pickup and shifted it smoothly into reverse, she gave every impression of being unaware of the sweaty cowboy who'd moved over only far enough for her to sit. She pretended not to notice that her right arm brushed his as she listened to one of the Langtry ranch hands direct her until she'd backed the stock trailer into position. She switched off the engine and was out the door so quickly that she'd spent a bit more than a minute behind the wheel.

Once out of the truck, she hurried to the back of the trailer. Two Langtry hands were pulling out the trailer ramp. The bull inside bellowed, and the sound seemed to make the trailer shiver. A heavy hoof pawed viciously at the trailer floor.

Rio climbed up the side of the board fence alley next to Boz, one of the older cowhands, and hooked a leg over the top rail.

"You want us to take that dumb sonofabuck out behind the barn and beat some manners into him, Miss Rio?"

Rio let out a tense breath and flashed the old cowhand a grateful smile. "Sounds good to me, but I

think we'll let it go by this time. Thanks, anyway.''
She returned her attention to the back of the trailer.

Once the ramp was out, both cowhands clambered
to the top rail of the fence. One gingerly reached
down from his high perch. Once he checked to make
certain the half dozen cowboys present were atop or
behind the fence, he unlatched the heavy door. He'd
just given the door a pull that would let it swing open
on its own when it suddenly burst wide.

The impact of the bull against the door was like a
crack of thunder. Rio started at the sudden boom as
did the other ranch hands. Kirby, the man who'd
opened the door, yelped and recoiled, balancing precariously atop the fence as he tried to cradle his injured hand. One of the men nearby reached over and
grabbed the back of his belt to keep him from falling
forward.

The bull rocketed out of the back of the trailer,
barreling down the narrow alley that angled him toward the gate of an empty corral. The ranch hand at
the corral shoved the gate closed the instant the bull
passed the opening.

Once inside, the outraged bull ran around the corral, charging anything he could see beyond the rails.
Rio jumped down from the fence, but instead of going
directly to the corral to check the bull, she hurried
toward the injured cowhand.

Kirby had climbed off the fence, and was leaning
against it while he cradled his wrist and hand against
his middle. His tanned face was pale and it was clear
to her that he was in pain.

"I'm sure sorry, Miss Rio. I was either a shade too slow or that bull was three shades too fast."

Rio touched his wrist and hand with gentle fingers as she carefully examined them. "You did fine, Kirby. But I think your wrist is broken." She carefully settled his arm back against his middle, then looked up into the young cowhand's strained features. "We'll get you some ice and have someone drive you to the hospital. Hank?" Rio turned her head to look for the other young cowhand. Hank started quickly toward them, but Rio redirected him with a brisk, "Would you go down to the cook house for some ice? Have Smitty call the hospital and tell them you're bringing Kirby in."

The cowhand ran toward the cook house and Rio turned Kirby over to one of the other men to escort him to the ranch pickup parked under a shade tree in the drive.

From there, she strode toward the corral where the bull was, unconcerned that the cowhand from the Cameron Ranch hovered impatiently by his pickup. She stopped next to Boz, who was shaking his head and swearing beneath his breath.

"Let's hope that A-bomb on hooves is showing such a sweet disposition because he don't travel good," the old cowhand remarked, "or because Cameron's man stirred him up."

Rio watched the bull closely, checking for any sign of injury. "Yeah, let's hope," she said quietly. Most bulls were volatile and temperamental, but there was something about this bull that made her uneasy. Boz had apparently sensed it, too. On the other hand, Kirby's injury might be influencing both of them.

Besides, Kane had selected this bull himself. The bull's superior quality and impressive pedigree would make him an ideal addition to Langtry's breeding program. If he could be managed, the animal was invaluable.

As if the bull had sensed her misgivings, he shifted directions in the enclosure. In the next moment, he charged straight for her like a steam engine at full throttle. Rio stiffened on her side of the fence, but didn't move. If the bull was loco enough to challenge the sturdy wood posts and heavy rails of this corral, it was better to know right away.

The last few strides of the huge animal were truly terrifying. Boz stepped aside, as if he didn't trust the fence would hold against the power of the bull. It was at the last second—when Rio was about to give in to the instinct to jump aside herself—that the big bull slid to a dusty halt a mere hand span from the rails. His huge head went down and he pawed so furiously at the dirt that he made furrows in the hard-packed surface.

The hoots and whistles of the cowhands who'd been watching were as much male admiration for the bull's bravado as it was relief that he'd shown he would respect a fence.

It wouldn't have occurred to Rio that the nerve she'd just shown was at least a part of that male admiration. She turned from the fence and walked back to where the cowhand who'd delivered the bull waited.

The cowboy's insolent expression was back, letting her know that he had no intention of showing a female in authority much respect. Either he didn't know or it didn't matter to him that she regularly acted in Kane's stead concerning Langtry business.

Rio's authority had been challenged before by cowboys whose egos were too frail to take orders from a woman. Few of them worked on Langtry, and this cowboy worked for someone else.

She forced her mouth into a polite line that wouldn't be mistaken for a smile. "If Mr. Langtry buys more stock from your boss, volunteer for some other chore and let him send someone more professional to Langtry. Have a safe trip."

Rio delivered the advice in a mild tone, then walked past the cowhand to check on Kirby. It was well known that Langtry hospitality always included an invitation for a meal or, at the very least, sandwiches and cold drinks or coffee for anyone who came through the front gate. The fact that Rio hadn't extended that hospitality to the cowboy was a setdown and would be taken as such. Particularly by the cowboy's employer if he found out.

Rio had just rounded the front of the cowboy's truck when she saw Kane standing next to the passenger side of the pickup where Kirby waited for Hank to return with some ice. She continued toward him, then gave Kirby a gentle smile as she stopped by the open truck door next to Kane. "How're you doin', cowboy?"

"Not bad, Miss Rio," he answered, and gave her a tight grin.

Rio nodded past them at Hank who was jogging over from the cook house with two large bags of ice and a pair of folded towels. "Hank's coming right now."

When Hank reached the truck, Rio wrapped the ice bags in the towels and positioned them carefully around Kirby's wrist and hand. Kane's ongoing silence, aside from a few words to Kirby, gave Rio the clear impression that he wasn't pleased with her.

But then, he could see for himself that the Cameron cowhand was leaving. As they both stepped back and the Langtry pickup pulled away, Rio steeled herself for Kane's criticism and felt the inevitable dip of her insides when he didn't keep her waiting.

"You didn't offer Langtry hospitality to Ty's man."

Rio turned to him and lifted her chin in subtle defiance. "It was my decision to make. If you disagree..." Rio hesitated, submission to Kane tasting bitter. "I'll chase him down and bring him back."

Kane's harsh expression didn't alter, but his blue eyes burned down into hers. "Like hell you will."

Rio's lips parted in surprise before she swiftly recovered herself.

Kane glanced away from her and growled, "Disrespect toward you is a challenge of my authority to put you in charge."

"I appreciate that, Kane," she said. "Thanks."

Kane's gaze streaked back to impale hers. "It doesn't have a damned thing to do with you."

Rio's breath caught at his sudden hostility, but she forced her mouth into a curve that she hoped concealed her dismay. "I'm sure I could figure that out for myself," she said, then gave him a mock salute as she started to back away. "I'm going up to see if Sam needs anything," she added, then turned to walk to the house, hoping she could escape before Kane could voice any other unpleasantness.

CHAPTER THREE

RAMONA and Tracy arrived on Langtry at four o'clock that afternoon. They'd flown from Dallas that morning with neighboring rancher, Deke Sanderson, in his private plane, but instead of landing at Langtry's airstrip, they'd touched down at the Sanderson ranch.

Though Rio secretly disapproved of Ramona's and Tracy's hours-long visit with the widowed rancher, she kept her thoughts to herself. Their return to Langtry would likely prove difficult enough once Ramona realized that Rio would be at the main house.

Rio allowed them the time between their late-afternoon arrival and supper to catch up with Sam and Kane and to get settled in. Because their homecoming was considered an occasion, Rio set aside her usual choice of jeans and a blouse in favor of a blue sundress and sandals before she came down to supper.

She entered the living room where everyone but Sam waited for Ardis to announce supper. Tracy sat at one end of the sofa and Ramona stood with Kane in front of the liquor cabinet. Rio walked toward a wing chair at the edge of the formal furniture grouping in front of the stone fireplace. Ramona was the first to see her arrive.

"Ah, here's Rio now, Kane, just as you said," Ramona announced, and immediately flashed Rio a saccharine smile. "Kane is mixing drinks," she told Rio. "Would you like him to fix you something?"

"No, thank you," Rio murmured, and sat down.

Ramona nodded sagely and gave Rio a sympathetic look. "A wise choice for you, my dear, considering."

Rio tensed at the bald reference to her father's alcoholism but sat back in her chair and pretended not to have noticed. She glanced toward Tracy who hadn't acknowledged her yet. Two years younger than Rio's twenty-three, Tracy was a small, delicate blonde like her mother, with huge blue eyes and a flawless complexion. Tracy was usually as sweet as her mother was witchy. When Tracy glanced her way, Rio gave her a soft smile. "Hello, Tracy."

Tracy's, "Hello," was plainly obligatory. She immediately turned from Rio, her manner cool and unfriendly.

Taken aback by Tracy's snub, Rio glanced Kane's way as he left the liquor cabinet and came toward the sofa to sit down with his drink. His hard gaze met hers, then moved appraisingly over her sundress and down the smooth length of her legs before it shifted away. It wasn't the kind of look she usually got from Kane, and Rio's self-consciousness escalated.

Sam came into the room shortly after, just before Ardis called them to the meal. Sam offered his arm to Ramona, who cooed with exaggerated pleasure and glided to his side in a cloud of chiffon and perfume. Sam offered his other arm to Tracy and escorted both women into the dining room.

That left Rio with Kane, creating an awkwardness that made her squirm inwardly. Kane usually managed to avoid being paired with her socially, whether it was at some grand occasion or something as simple as escorting her from one room to the next with company present. She couldn't believe Sam had put either of them on the spot, particularly since he knew how Kane felt about her.

Suddenly deciding to spare them both, Rio started to follow Sam and the others. She'd not gone more than two steps past Kane before his hard, strong fingers closed around her arm and brought her to a halt. Rio turned toward him in surprise. His handsome features were as harsh as ever, his blue eyes glinting with irritation.

Meanwhile, the firm grip on her arm was sending a tide of sensation through her. The memory of the kiss in the stable came flooding back, shocking her with the sudden craving to be kissed again.

"Sam expects me to do the gentlemanly thing by you," Kane was saying before his mouth curved with a mixture of amusement and mockery. "And if Ramona could see your face right now, she'd give you a tongue-lashing that would cut you to ribbons."

Rio stiffened and tried to free her arm. Kane tightened his grip and tugged her closer. She braced a hand against his chest to maintain the narrow distance between them. Her defiant, "Leave me alone, Kane," was a bit breathless.

"Then keep those soft, hungry looks to yourself." The low words were brutal.

Her face flushed. She gave him a shove that should have pushed him away, but he stood before her like a granite column. The heat from his shirtfront seared her palm, the steady rhythm of the heart beneath her hand beating once for every two beats of her own. She was suddenly overwhelmed by his maleness, and staggered by the powerful longings of her own body.

What a fool she was! Self-preservation won out over desire and gave her the strength to push away from Kane and step back. She couldn't look him in the eye, but she felt the laser intensity of his gaze as she turned and walked swiftly toward the dining room.

She was so attuned to him that she heard every unhurried boot step as he followed. And though she avoided looking at him during the meal, she sensed every move he made, and felt it like a touch each time he looked at her.

At least Ramona allowed her to eat her meal in peace. Rio began to think the older woman's attitude toward her had mellowed, which put her a little more at ease. It wasn't until later that she realized Ramona hadn't mellowed a bit.

They had all moved back into the living room. Ardis was carrying in a coffee tray. Sam had excused himself for an early night. Ramona barely waited long enough for the elevator at the back hall to reach the upstairs level before she began.

"Sam's been quite charitable toward you all these years, Rio." Ramona's voice was soft and sweetly modulated, but her words were like a slap.

Rio hesitated as she reached for the coffee cup Ardis passed her. The old shame that burst up made her break contact with Ardis's watchful gaze as she took the cup and saucer.

She didn't respond to Ramona's opening salvo. Kane would take a dim view of any verbal retaliation on her part, and perhaps Ardis felt the same way. Ardis had never been particularly friendly toward her, so Rio didn't think of her as an ally.

As if she were flaunting the knowledge that no one in the room would object, Ramona went on. "I'd think you'd have more pride than to keep hanging around, playing up to that poor old man in hopes of getting more out of him."

Rio sipped her coffee as she struggled to conceal her anger. Any sign of upset would please Ramona, and Rio was determined to thwart her. She lowered her cup and calmly met the malicious gleam in Ramona's eyes. "Sam's no fool, Ramona."

Beneath her quiet words was a warning to Ramona about the infidelity Rio suspected her of. She doubted the others in the room would take those words at anything but face value, but Ramona took them exactly as Rio had intended. There was no mistaking the wild flush of outrage that colored her flawless face.

Ramona turned toward Kane who grimly watched them both. "Can't you do something about her, Kane?"

Kane's mouth quirked in faint sarcasm. "What is it you want me to do, Ramona?"

"Fire her, make her leave—" she waved one hand impatiently "—whatever it takes."

Rio set her cup aside, her nerves going painfully tight as she prepared to rise and leave the room. She shouldn't have stayed for coffee, she never should have hung around once Sam had retired for the evening. She'd lived on Langtry long enough to know how things were and how they would always be.

"Finish your coffee, Rio." Kane's rough drawl carried the steely undertone of an order. She glanced up, but Kane's blue gaze was fixed on Ramona.

"Rio earns her keep, Ramona. And since she works for me, I'd appreciate it if you'd let me decide whether she's out of line or not."

Ramona's perfect face was suddenly the picture of dismay. "Kane..." she hesitated, clearly confused. "Surely you aren't—"

"Leave it alone." Kane's icy tone cut her off.

Ramona's mouth rounded in surprise, but she quickly affected a wounded look. Kane appeared oblivious to the act as he turned his attention to Tracy. Rio could only stare, as shocked by Kane's unexpected intervention as Ramona was.

The excitement that stormed over her when she realized that Kane had actually defended her ebbed swiftly. He wasn't really sticking up for her, he was responding to a challenge to his authority. And, as he'd said that morning, it had nothing to do with her.

Rio picked up her cup, but was no longer interested in coffee. She could feel the hostility that radiated from Ramona as Kane made small talk with Tracy. She rose to her feet with unhurried grace to set her cup and saucer on the tray, then slipped out of the room while Kane was distracted by his conversation with his stepsister.

She might have made good the escape to her room, but the doorbell rang. Since she was closer to the front of the house than either Ardis or Estelle, she took a quick detour to answer the door.

B.J. Hastings waited on the doorstep. Peacock handsome, his blond hair and blue eyes made him look almost angelic. Though he was almost as tall as Kane, his lean body didn't carry the hard muscle that Kane's did. But then, even though Kane managed several Langtry business interests, he still did ranch work with surprising regularity. B.J., she knew, enjoyed being the boss when his father left him in charge, but he wouldn't have dreamed of working with his men. He often chided her for working with the Langtry ranch hands, vacillating between horror and careful ridicule depending on the work Rio was doing at the time.

And that was just one of the many reasons Rio found him lacking as a marriage prospect.

"Hello, darlin'," he drawled, his eyes wandering down her slim body with open appreciation. "Any chance we've got the house to ourselves tonight?"

Rio managed a soft smile and a quiet "Hello," secretly unhappy about the question. She ignored it and said, "Come out to the kitchen. It's a little less crowded there." She turned and led the way, quickly passing the wide doorway into the living room. She heard B.J.'s irritable murmur as he tried to keep up.

Ardis and Estelle were in the kitchen, a Scrabble game laid out on the table in the breakfast nook as they watched a network news program. Disappointed that the room wasn't free, she smiled at the two women and continued on out the back door to the patio as if that had been their destination all along.

She went to one of the shadowy areas near the far end of the pool before she stopped. B.J. caught up to her, then took her arm and turned her toward him. In the next second his open mouth swooped down on hers as his arms tightened like bands around her.

Warm and wet, his mouth was not firm but soft, as if he were smearing it over her lips. Coming so soon after Kane's steamy kiss, Rio couldn't help noticing the difference. She also couldn't help that B.J.'s kiss repulsed her.

As quickly as she could, she managed to pull back, privately appalled that B.J. compared so unfavorably to Kane.

"Ah, come on, Rio," B.J. groaned, then tried unsuccessfully to recapture her lips with his. Rio braced her hands against his chest to create some space, but his mouth found the side of her neck. "Girls like you are supposed to be wild and willing," he murmured as he nibbled the delicate flesh. His marauding lips were repellent, but his words were chilling.

Rio gave him a shove that gained her freedom, then took a step back. Something in her rigid posture discouraged him from reaching for her a second time.

"Girls like me?" she asked quietly. "What about girls like me?"

Though his face was heavily shadowed, Rio could see that B.J. was too annoyed with her to realize he was treading on shaky ground. He answered with a foolish lack of caution.

"Yeah, girls like you." Frustration made him give the words a faint sneer. "Beautiful, come-from-nothin' girls who know how to play up to big money. Only in your case, you never try too hard.''

Rio stared, not really surprised by the insult. She'd known much of B.J.'s attention was an act, she'd sensed it from the first. It was because of his sudden attention and her less than exalted status in their community that she'd not immediately rebuffed him. Somehow, things had rapidly escalated, until B.J.'s surprise proposal had left her scrambling for a way to turn him down without offending him. She should have known it was inevitable.

Her soft, ''I think you'd better leave,'' sounded as calm as she could make it, but she was trembling with anger.

B.J. cocked his head as if he hadn't heard correctly. ''What did you say?''

The deep voice that intruded startled them both. ''I heard what she said, Hastings, and I'm standing over here.''

Rio turned and saw Kane standing across the pool from them in the deep shadow of the stone wall. ''Give your daddy our regards.''

It was a blatant invitation to leave. B.J. stood there a moment, his hands clenching and unclenching at his sides, before he spun away and headed toward the patio gate and the sidewalk that would take him to the front driveway.

Rio watched him go, more relieved by Kane's intrusion than she wanted to admit. The problem of how to deal with B.J.'s proposal had just been solved, and she didn't care that she hadn't been the one to solve it. She could not, however, let Kane know she appreciated his intrusion.

She looked toward the deep shadows across the pool at Kane.

"Spying?" she asked, forcing just the right touch of challenge into her tone.

"Looking out for Langtry interests. Saving B.J. a world of sexual frustration." He paused a moment before his voice went rough. "I told you to tell him no."

Rio was grateful for the dimness that concealed the heat in her face. The memory of how Kane had been touching her when he'd first said those words sent a torrent of longing through her. Somehow she made her voice sound strong. "I take your orders where the ranch is concerned, Kane. You don't have any say in my personal business."

"We won't argue about that tonight, Rio. You're done with B.J. I hope you're smart enough to keep it that way."

She stared warily into the darkness that concealed him, as mystified by his sudden intrusion into her personal life as she was by his intervention with Ramona earlier.

On the other hand, he'd said he was looking out for Langtry interests. Only a fool would take that blunt statement at more than face value—particularly since it was Kane who'd said it.

Before she could respond to his autocratic remarks he was gone, striding toward the back door to the kitchen, his brisk manner emphasizing the emotional distance between them.

* * *

Rio wasn't eager to leave the house after breakfast that next morning. Sam seemed more tired than usual, weaker. She'd seen him take one of his tiny pills at the table, but a frown from Kane made her conceal her worry.

In a departure from the norm, she and Kane lingered over coffee. Ramona and Tracy weren't awake yet, and it would be hours before either of them came downstairs for breakfast. In the end, it was Sam who sent them on their way, gruffly reminding them that they had responsibilities.

Rio was present when Kane discussed work with the foreman and their men, but as usual, she kept in the background. By the time he dismissed them, she realized that he hadn't assigned her anything in particular.

Kane waited until they stepped out of the cookhouse before he spoke to her. "I'll be in the office this morning. Find something to do until you think Ramona and Tracy have had time to come downstairs and finish breakfast. Come see me after that." His eyes met hers solemnly, and Rio had the startling sense that he was including her as his equal in their vigil over his father's health. "Unless I send for you sooner."

The words made her heart sink, but she nodded. "I'll be close by."

They went their separate ways, Kane to his office, Rio to one of the stables to work with a colt she'd been training. A feeling of foreboding wound around her heart. The minutes crawled along until at last it was time to go to the house.

* * *

Sam Langtry couldn't remember being too young to ride a horse. His daddy had bragged that his fine, strapping son had ridden in front of him in the saddle by the time he was strong enough to hold up his head, taking the reins in his chubby little hands by the time he was nine months old. Since all that was true, it was no wonder that not riding a horse for the past year had seemed so damned unnatural.

The old red roan gelding nudged his arm as if to remind him of the sugar cube he'd promised. Sam dug into his shirt pocket and brought out the treat. His hands were shaking so from weariness that he almost lost the cube before he could hold it out in his palm.

He stepped to the horse's side and checked the cinch with expert hands before he gathered the reins. He got his foot in the stirrup and swung himself upward, alarmed at how much strength was required to mount, but pleased that the movement still felt as natural to him as breathing.

Once he was atop the old horse, the pain in his chest sharpened. Dizziness made him feel sick and his breath came hard. The vial of pills he was never without was in his pocket, and he went for a last dose with weak fingers.

It took so long to feel better that he began to worry that he might pass out before he could get clear of the stable door. He was hurting, but at least he'd got the saddle on Spinner before it had got this bad. Despite the pain and that odd kind of wooziness, he felt better than he had in a long time.

At his signal, the roan stepped forward as if he, too, were eager to head out like old times. Sam had been hoping Spinner's gait was still as smooth as he remembered, and to his relief, it was. He relaxed as the familiarity of being on horseback gave him a reviving feeling of youth.

He and Spinner moved sedately down one of the alleys that bisected the network of corrals. If anyone had seen him, they sure hadn't tried to stop him. He released a cautious breath when they cleared the headquarters and the only thing before them was the massive, sun-bright Langtry range.

Rio was walking up the path from the shaded corral she left the colt in. Out of habit, she scanned what she could see of the headquarters and the open land beyond. At first, she didn't pay undue attention to the tall cowboy she saw ride through the last gate toward the range. The sight was so familiar to her that what she was seeing didn't fully register until she was about to glance away.

It seemed odd that someone was taking Spinner out. The roan cowpony was Sam's, but Sam had long ago retired him. They'd brought him in from the range a month ago to doctor an infected cut, but some of the kids around the ranch had been as drawn to the old horse as he was to them. Kane had decided to allow them to ride the cowpony for the summer as long as they were easy on him and didn't bother him during the heat of the day.

And that was why it was so strange to see one of the ranch hands riding him out to work. Rio's steps slowed as she continued to stare, struck by the notion that she was seeing Sam ride away from the headquarters as tall and strong as ever. And when the cowboy reached up to adjust his hat, the familiarity of the gesture confirmed it.

Panic jolted her into movement, sending her running for the main house and Kane.

Sam and Spinner made it to the tree-scattered rise of the Painted Fence. Sam's elation at escaping the ranch headquarters on horseback was probably all that kept him from folding over with the terrible pain in his chest.

Lord, it was good to be out in the open, a warm wind on his face, a solid horse beneath him and all of Langtry spread around him like a vast kingdom. He hadn't wanted to die in a hospital, he hadn't wanted to die indoors. He'd wanted to die like this, exactly like this, natural, without fuss, beneath the Texas sky with the sight and sound and smell of the land around him.

He let Spinner walk up to the hitch rail just outside the white picket fence that surrounded the family cemetery. The old horse came to a halt and stood patiently.

Sam managed to dismount, barely able to hold on to the saddle long enough for his buckling knees to steady. The pain that was cleaving his chest made him feel weak as a baby, but he forced himself forward. Once he was inside the gate, he made his way past the assortment of gravestones.

His first wife, Marlie, wasn't buried here. She'd died of pneumonia the spring Kane had turned two, and her mama had wanted her buried with the rest of her family in a cemetery near Dallas. Sam had given in out of pity for his mother-in-law-of three years.

He was almost glad now that Marlie wasn't resting here, though he'd loved her with the intensity of a newlywed husband. If she were, he would have been obliged to leave instructions that he be buried beside her. As it was, he meant to be buried next to Lenore Cory.

It'd been easy to get Ned Cory's agreement to bury his wife on Langtry, easy because Sam had offered to pay all the costs for the casket, headstone and funeral. But two years later, when Ned Cory had died in the car crash, Sam'd had him interred in the county cemetery ten miles away.

No one had ever questioned Sam about the arrangements for either funeral, and he himself had never remarked upon it to anyone. He'd been in love with another man's wife. The moral torment of that had kept him from taking her away from Cory while she was alive; it hadn't kept him from keeping her away from Cory after her death. Besides, it had seemed right for Lenore to be here, right for little Rio to be able to have her mama's grave near enough to take flowers to.

Sam almost reached the lovely headstone at Lenore's grave before the very last of his strength began to wane. He didn't make it to the shade before he collapsed.

"God, Rio, don't tell me you've come in to hang around the house." Ramona made a face as Rio rushed past her from the back door. Rio was in such a hurry to find Kane that Ramona barely made an impression. She raced down the back hall and charged into Kane's office.

Her breathless, "Where's Sam?" was choked. Kane glanced up, took in her pale face, then returned his attention to the stack of papers before him.

"He's been in bed since after breakfast," he told her. "Doc Kady's coming out for lunch so he can check on him."

Rio shook her head. "I just saw him take Spinner out."

Kane grunted. "He's not well enough to ride, Rio, you know that."

"Then explain how he did it," she blurted.

Ramona stood in the open doorway. "Kane, why do you allow her to speak to you in that tone?"

Kane didn't answer either of them, but fired a question at Ramona. "Is Sam still upstairs?"

Ramona seemed surprised, but shook her head. "No, he said he was going down to the stable. His color wasn't the best, so I thought it would do him good to get some sun."

Rio felt a surge of rage she could barely contain. It was just like Ramona to think in such a superficial way about the seriousness of Sam's illness. Kane was on his feet in an instant, coming quickly around the desk before he suddenly stopped and turned back for the cell phone beside the lamp.

An instant later they were both running through the house to the back door. Kane slowed long enough to order Estelle, "Check the house for Sam. If you find him, call me right away on the cell phone. If you don't, call Doc Kady, tell him we think Dad's gone riding, and have him come out early.''

They both were out the door and halfway across the patio before Estelle could reply.

CHAPTER FOUR

THE heat reminded Sam of that first day. He'd been riding the bad manners out of a green-broke colt and had ended up checking the fence along the south highway. He'd seen the old brown pickup, seen the back end sagging under the weight of mismatched furniture and cowboy tack. One of the front tires was flat.

Then he'd seen the woman. Tall and willowy, she wore her dark hair wound up in a loose knot. The blue flowered dress she'd had on belled and fluttered in the light breeze. She'd been balancing a sleeping baby on one slim hip and she'd lifted a hand to shade her eyes when she caught sight of his approach.

He'd drawn the colt to a halt at the fence. She'd smiled at him then, a sweet, shy, nervous little smile that had got him by the heart. He'd tipped his hat, then dismounted and tied the colt to the fence.

Neither he nor the woman said a word to each other until he'd crossed the shallow ditch. As he got closer, he saw that her lovely eyes were a breathtaking blue. Her face was delicate, her nose and high cheekbones already turning pink from the sun. The one-year-old she balanced on her hip was a rosy-cheeked cherub of a child, her small dark head on her mama's shoulder, sound asleep.

Sam reckoned then that he'd never seen a more lovely sight. The beauty and her babe. And as he'd looked into her remarkable eyes, he'd seen the sweetness, the tender spirit of her, the loneliness and the lifetime of yearning he'd felt in his own heart...

The pain in his chest almost made him pass out. Sam forced himself to stay conscious, unwilling to let go of the memories until he came to the one he loved most...

Lenore, working in her garden behind the little house her family lived in on Langtry. She'd grown flowers around the neat plot of vegetables. Beautiful flowers. Some she'd dug from a pasture and reset, some she'd grown from dime store seed. More than a dozen different kinds, dozens of colors and hues.

She'd had on a faded housedress with no sleeves. She'd been barefoot, walking among the profusion of blooms without crushing a single stem. Carefully, tenderly, she'd been clipping off a bloom stalk here and there, adding to the rich bouquet she'd been gathering.

She'd looked up to see him, smiled that tender Madonna smile, and started toward where he stood, hat in hand, at the edge of her garden. She'd shyly thanked him, for at least the tenth time, for allowing her to plant a garden. He'd gallantly told him that if he hadn't needed to graze cattle he might have had the whole of Langtry plowed so she could grow flowers.

That's when she told him she'd been picking the bouquet for him. "For some brightness in your day, Sam," she'd said in her quiet, shy way. "The sweet smells and colors always give my heart a lift. I surely hope you might enjoy them, too."

Oh, God, he had! He could still feel the feather-light brush of her slim fingers as he'd taken the flowers. The lump in his throat had about strangled him, but he'd managed to thank her, even as his heart clenched with love and need and despair.

Because he could never have her. He'd struggled with the agony of the moral dilemma, struggled to contain his feelings, struggled not to beat hell out of her husband for not appreciating how lucky he was.

And he'd kept that bouquet. He'd bought the biggest, heaviest book he could find in Austin, and he'd pressed every blossom in its pages. No bloom had been too frail, no petal too small. He'd left the book for Rio...

"Sam?"

Lenore's voice was barely audible above the pain. "Sam?"

He could feel her cool palm on his cheek. Only because he thought it was Lenore did he open his eyes. The haze of pain eased enough for him to see that it was Rio, and his emotions rose again as he noted her distress.

"You're her image," he managed to tell her.

He felt the tremor in her hand as she stroked his forehead. Her tearful, "Please, Sam," carried an edge of pain that he expected. God, he hated that after everything Rio had meant to him over the years, that he was going to end up hurting her.

He was glad to see Kane with her, relieved that their concern for him was bringing them together. They each had taken hold of his hands and he wondered if either of them knew how wonderful it was to touch them, to feel the vitality of their youth and the power of their love for him one last time.

The sun must have gone behind a cloud bank. Sam welcomed the dimmer light, welcomed the gust of coolness that swept him. The pain in his chest was still intense, but there was an odd numbness that made it more bearable.

It took so much for him to get the words out. "Love you both. Take care of each other," he whispered. "The letters...say for me..."

The last pain didn't hurt so much as it paralyzed. Sam was looking up into the two faces he loved most when his eyelids grew too heavy. His last breath eased away and took the pain with it.

Rio stared in disbelief as she watched Sam's eyes close and felt his weak grip go slack. Grief settled so heavily in her chest that she thought at first the pressure would crush her.

Tears blurred her eyes, but not so much that she couldn't lean over and place one last kiss on Sam's cheek. She laid his hand reverently across his middle, painfully aware of Kane.

Somehow she made herself turn from Sam and get to her feet so she could take a few steps away. Shock made her feel dazed and sluggish. The reminder that Sam was the only person she could have safely shared this terrible grief with made her feel even more desolate.

She wrapped her arms around herself, and when the first spasm of sobs came, she couldn't get control of them for a few moments. She jumped when she felt

Kane's big hand settle on her shoulder. The compulsion to turn to him and fling herself into his arms was so strong suddenly that she shook with the effort to control the impulse.

It was a relief when she heard him speak quietly into the cell phone. His attention wasn't on her, and his distraction gave her more time to compose herself.

It was the warm weight of Kane's hand, or rather, the deceptively consoling feel of it, that made Rio ease away and walk through the gate to where Spinner waited at the hitch rail. She and Kane had brought the Suburban. Once some of the men arrived, they would take Sam home in the back of the big vehicle.

Spinner gave her a gentle nudge. Rio stroked the old cowpony's head, then fought a new flood of tears when the horse pushed his head against her as if he, too, were grieving for an old friend. Rio wrapped an arm around the horse's neck and hugged him.

The sound of a ranch pickup was almost welcome. Rio turned and glanced over her shoulder toward it. Kane was standing between her and the oncoming truck. Her gaze connected with the bleakness in his, then veered away.

"Come on, Rio," Kane said, his big voice sounding odd, choked. "Someone else can bring Spinner in."

For a moment, Kane thought she'd refuse. She nodded and he watched as she drew herself up straighter, tighter. He could see she was still shaking. She looked as shell-shocked as he felt, and though she managed to control her tears, he could see the stark grief in the wild shine of her eyes.

Sam was laid gently on a pallet in the back of the Suburban, his black Stetson resting over his face. Kane and Rio rode on either side of his body. By the time they arrived at the headquarters, it was noon. The ambulance had already arrived.

Rio couldn't watch as Doc Kady directed the transfer to the ambulance. She felt chilled, and the restlessness she felt made it almost impossible to stand still. It seemed every ranch hand on the place was there, hat in hand, looking on soberly.

When at last the ambulance pulled slowly away, Kane started for the house. Rio automatically followed, then hesitated. Now that Sam was gone, there wasn't a person at the main house who wanted her around. The desolation she felt was compounded by the worry that Kane might expect her to leave the ranch as soon as possible.

The reminder that she'd not only lost Sam but her home and her place in the world filled her with dread. The anguish she felt overwhelmed her and she turned from the house, so restless and unsettled inside she thought she might fly apart.

Instinct drove her to hide, to vent her grief in private, until the worst of it was over and she found the courage to face what was ahead. She'd done that when her mother died, and later when her father was killed. There were several safe places on the ranch, beautiful solitary places that she might never see again once Sam was laid to rest and she was finally banished from Langtry. She could find them all one last time and say goodbye to them just as she somehow had to say goodbye to Sam.

Indecision made her waver only a moment more before she was rushing toward the stables and the sanctuary of the land.

"Do you know where the will is?"

Ramona's question stunned him. Kane had just told her that her husband had passed away. Ardis and Estelle were already crying, and Tracy was teary-eyed, but Ramona's first response was to ask if he knew where Sam's will was.

He saw the flash of horror in her beautiful eyes when she realized her gaffe, and she scrambled to recover herself. "Won't you need it right away to ensure a smooth transition of ownership? I mean, there must be a million legalities with the ranch and all those holdings and investments. I—I'm certain your father wouldn't want you to be further upset at a time like this."

"That's right, Ramona, he wouldn't," Kane said bluntly, then abruptly turned to leave the room.

But Ramona stepped in front of him and pushed her way into his arms, doing an elegant job of dissolving into the teary show of grief that had been a bit long in coming. Kane automatically put his arms around her, but he tolerated her delicate sniffles only a few moments before he set her away from himself and left the room.

Rio didn't come back to the headquarters until after dark the next evening. The desolation she felt had kept her riding over the Langtry range for hours at a stretch. She'd stopped periodically to water her horse and unsaddle it to graze, but shock and restlessness pushed her to keep moving, keep riding, in an attempt to make it ease.

At last, dazed by exhaustion and hunger, she rode back to the stable. She took care of grooming her horse, then turned him into a stall with fresh water and a generous measure of grain. On the walk to the house, she slowly became aware of the number of cars and pickups that virtually clogged the ranch drive and covered the lawn around the house.

Panicked by the sight that promised a houseful of guests, she changed course and circled the lawn, hoping to slip unnoticed into the kitchen from the patio. She couldn't face so many people in her present state. Besides, Sam wouldn't be there now. Without him to ensure her acceptance, Rio wasn't certain she wanted to put anyone's real feelings toward her to the test.

She made it into the kitchen, relieved that no one was there. Ardis and Estelle were probably waiting on guests, so she hurried to the back hall and the stairs.

She didn't escape unseen, but was forced to give a small wave of acknowledgment to two ladies from church who were carrying empty trays back to the kitchen. The surprise on their faces made her flush self-consciously, but she rushed up the stairs then along the hall to the safety of her room.

Once there, she closed the door. She didn't turn on the lights, but tossed her hat toward a chair and made her way across the room by memory. She entered her bathroom and sat down tiredly on the edge of the tub. The murmur of voices from downstairs was faint, but she could hear them. She leaned forward and braced her elbows on her knees. She combed her fingers into her hair and rested her forehead wearily on the heels of her hands.

The church ladies' surprise was probably fright. After most of two days and a night on the range in the dust and wind and heat, she knew she was a sight. She was just working up the energy to stand and get undressed for a hot bath when a loud pounding started on her bedroom door.

She jerked her head up, but before she could call out, the door swung inward. Kane's tall, broad-shouldered body blocked the light from the hall momentarily before he stepped in and flipped the light switch. Once he looked across into her bathroom and saw her sitting on the edge of the tub, he shut the door with a snap.

"Where the hell have you been?" he demanded.

Rio thought she had her emotions under control—she'd cried until she was numb—but the moment Kane snarled at her, the misery she'd worked so hard to distance herself from came flooding back.

"You look like hell," he went on as he stalked toward her and stepped over the threshold into her bath. He mercilessly switched on the light and Rio winced from the brightness.

"I feel like hell, too, Kane. Leave me alone."

Kane stared down in private horror. Rio was a mess. She was all-over dust, her unbound hair looked like a hip-length tangle of witch's hair, but the desolation in her eyes was frightening. He thought about Ramona downstairs, her hair perfectly coifed, her makeup just so, and wearing an elegant black dress.

She was carrying a black lace hankie around as a prop, but as far as he was concerned, her grief was playacting compared to Rio's.

He lowered himself to a crouch before her and Rio instantly turned her head. She'd started shaking again, he noted, and he could tell from her tense profile that she was biting her lower lip hard enough to draw blood.

"Think you could eat something hot if I brought it up to you?"

If Kane's harsh tone upset the frail control she had over her emotions, his gentle drawl blew it to smithereens. The breath she'd been slowly exhaling suddenly jerked back in on a sob. She sprang to her feet and tried to step past him. Kane stood and blocked her way.

"Damn it, Kane—why are you—mean—then nice?" Rio got out around the series of sobs, then covered her face with both hands, mortified that she was crying in front of him.

"Because I worried about you," he growled.

His answer was so unexpected that Rio lowered her hands to look at him, her tear-filled eyes wide. As if he'd been waiting for her complete attention, he went on brutally.

"But I don't want to worry about you, do you understand?" He leaned aggressively toward her and she drew back, dismayed that his wonderful confession had been dashed. He caught her wrists to halt her retreat. "I don't want to worry about you. I don't want to think about you—I don't want to feel the things I feel when I look at you."

Rio stared at the fierceness on his handsome face, cut to her soul by his angry words. She looked away from him and gave a small, stiff nod, her heart so heavy with the added grief Kane's words caused her that she was amazed she didn't die.

Her whispered, "All right, Kane, I get the message," was barely audible.

Kane gave her a small shake that brought her dispirited gaze back to his. "No, you don't, Rio. You don't get it at all."

He let go of her then, but slowly. The turmoil in his eyes riveted her. Either she was too exhausted to break contact, or she was mesmerized by his intensity. His hand came up briefly to her cheek, the tender caress part consolation, part apology.

It was Kane who ended those tense moments for them both. He turned abruptly from her and stormed toward the door, leaving her room just as suddenly and forcefully as he'd entered it.

Rio's appearance at breakfast the next morning was a necessity. Kane had brought a tray of food to her room last night while she was in the tub, but she'd only picked at it. She wasn't certain she could eat much now, but because she'd gone most of the past two days without food, she knew she had to try. Kane was already at the table. He glanced up when she entered the dining room. Rio sat down, quietly thanked him for the tray he'd brought up, but neither of them said anything more to disrupt the pall of silence in the big room.

Ardis maintained the silence as she served breakfast, but to Rio's surprise, the cook gave her shoulder a gentle pat as she set her plate in front of her. The small gesture had been unexpected and, as Rio was finding, kindness made it more difficult for her to keep her emotions in check.

"Did you sleep?" Kane's brusque question disturbed the tense silence.

Rio shook her head, then decided to bring up the subject she'd been mulling over. She couldn't look at him. "I know I haven't been around to do my share the past two days. But since I'll be leaving after the funeral, I thought I might as well use the day to get my things packed. You can dock my pay accordingly." She slid her fork under a fluffy corner of her scrambled eggs and lifted them off her plate.

"Are you quitting?"

Somehow his question made her feel in the wrong, as if she were running out on him, and she resented that. "I suppose you'd rather fire me," she guessed wearily. "Be my guest."

The silence that followed was ominous. She got the forkful of eggs to her mouth, but had to force herself to eat them. Though they tasted wonderful she had a terrible time getting them down.   When Kane tossed down his napkin and shoved his chair back, the violence of the action startled her. Rio kept herself from looking his way as he left the room, and sat frozen until she heard the back door slam.

She lowered her fork to her plate, no longer interested in food at all. She laid her napkin aside and rose to begin the sad task of collecting her things and preparing to leave.

Rio worked most of the morning moving the belongings she'd stored in the attic down to her room. About midmorning she went out to the attic space over the huge garage to search for the boxes of her mother's things that she and Sam had stored there.

There weren't many boxes. Lenore Cory had never been rich, never had many belongings. She'd owned only a few pieces of jewelry, none of it expensive. There was a shoe box of photographs, a baby book and a scrapbook of pictures. She found a box of legal and personal papers. There was even an old cookbook crammed with extra recipes her mother had clipped from magazines or written on recipe cards and bits of paper. Rio almost overlooked a box that held the small sewing chest and the hand-stitched quilt top she remembered her mother piecing together. There was also a box of her mother's dresses, one that held a very feminine Western hat and another with two handbags and a pair of black low-heeled pumps.

Something about those few boxes—that contained what remained of her mother's meager possessions— increased the weight of grief she felt. She carried them down from the top of the garage, then moved them into the house and got them up to her room.

By the time she'd gathered everything from both attics, it was time for lunch. She went downstairs, though she dreaded having to deal with anyone. The activity of the morning had given her another focus besides grief, but the full weight of it came back by the time she made it down to the dining room.

Rio hesitated in the doorway when she saw Ramona sitting opposite the head of the big table. Tracy sat midway down the table, and Kane was nowhere to be seen. Though Kane was more antagonist than ally, it surprised Rio to discover how much more at ease she might have felt had he been there.

Ramona glanced toward where Rio stood and gave her a spiteful smile. Tracy looked her way, too, but the indifference on her pretty face before she found a sudden interest in the fresh floral centerpiece on the big table made Rio feel like a nonentity. As usual, Ramona started in.

"You might as well come sit down, Rio," she invited, and made a weary sound as if she were resigned to some awful task. "Ardis and Estelle warned us you'd be in for lunch. They also said you were packing to leave, though I hardly dared hope until I saw you lugging in those boxes from the garage."

There was no reason for Rio to subject herself to a meal with Ramona. Her appetite was poor enough as it was. She shook her head. "Just looking for Kane." With that lie uttered smoothly enough, Rio retreated from the room, then took a circuitous route through the large house to the kitchen where Ardis was putting the finishing touches on the meal she was about to serve. Estelle was taking salads from the refrigerator.

"Do you mind if I eat out on the patio?" Rio asked Ardis.

Her quiet words got both women's attention at once. It was Estelle who said, "Ain't good for you to keep to yourself so much." Rio glanced away from the faint reproach on the housekeeper's face. The brusque remark landed hard on her tender feelings.

Ardis was looking at her as if she was waiting for her to change her mind.

Rio had rarely asked anything of the two women. When she'd first come to the big house, she'd been afraid of the dour sisters. She'd learned quickly that if she took care of her own room, did her own laundry and always carefully cleaned up after herself, the two women tolerated her presence well enough. Friendship was something neither one of them had hinted at, and Rio had never been presumptuous enough to make any overtures. As a result, she didn't know Estelle well enough to decipher the personal comment she'd just made about her behavior. Instead, she backed toward the door to the hall. "On second thought, I need to get into town to pick up a few things. I might as well get something there."

Rio turned and left the room too quickly for either woman to comment further. She dashed upstairs for her car keys and her purse, then hurried back down, exiting the front of the house to avoid everyone else.

CHAPTER FIVE

BY SUPPER that evening, Rio had returned from town and finished sorting the stack of boxes she'd stashed in her walk-in closet. She'd been down to the stable to locate any odds and ends of tack, then packed it in the large trunk in one of the tack rooms that held the rest of her gear. Because of the trunk's size and weight, she needed to leave it and her saddles in the stable until after she went to pick up the small U-Haul trailer she'd reserved for the next day.

The shock of losing Sam and having to leave the only home she'd ever known jarred her emotions every time she slowed in her efforts to gather her things and get them in order. The hour of inactivity she endured before the evening meal left her feeling edgy and emotional by the time she'd showered and changed and gone downstairs.

Ramona and Tracy were in the living room, so Rio waited in the hall. Kane arrived just after she did. His dark hair was still damp as if he, too, had just showered. In his Levi's and white shirt with its sleeves folded back, he looked even more darkly tanned and fit than normal. Despite her grief, Rio had a hard time keeping her eyes off him.

Fortunately, Ardis called them to the dining room before the moment became too awkward. Rio led the way, then silently took her usual chair down from the head of the table. Ramona sat at the other end, but instead of taking his father's place at the head of the table, Kane sat across from Rio as he normally did. Tracy—who usually sat next to Rio—now sat down next to Kane.

It was a departure from the norm, but Rio was careful not to let anyone see that she'd noticed. She was very aware of the sharp tension in the room, which only seemed to emphasize the fact that Sam's place at the table was empty.

After Ardis served, Ramona barely gave anyone a chance to taste their food before she began a fresh campaign against Rio.

"Will we *all* be riding in your car to the visitation tonight, Kane?"

Ramona gave the word "all" just enough emphasis to let everyone know that she not was not only talking about Rio, but hinting that the idea of Rio riding in the same car with the family was unacceptable.

Kane hesitated as he cut into his steak. His dark blue eyes came up and connected with Rio's for a heartbeat of time before he looked over at Ramona. "You and Tracy might as well take your car, Ramona. Andy washed and serviced it the day before you got back. Besides, Rio and I have other business to take care of."

Ramona's mouth rounded in a little *O* of surprise before she recovered. "What kind of business could the two of you possibly have at that time of night?" she scoffed gently. "Honestly, Kane, now that Sam's gone and she's leaving, why would you feel the need to include her in any kind of business, particularly on the night before your father's funeral?''

If Ramona didn't recognize the warning signs, Rio certainly did. Kane had paused after he got the piece of steak cut. His handsome features turned hard, and a dull flush crept along his cheekbones. His eyes were flat with disapproval when he looked toward Ramona.

"Since you've never been privy to the business end of Langtry, Ramona, I'd appreciate it if you wouldn't try to tell me when or with whom I can do business."

Ramona looked stricken, her beautiful eyes going misty. "Why of course, Kane, dear," she fluttered. "I wasn't trying to tell you what to do, exactly. No—I was merely reminding you that as far as I could see, there's no reason to burden yourself with Rio any longer."

Kane went utterly still at that, and his blue gaze began to glitter. He didn't say another word, but then, he didn't have to. Ramona grew genuinely fretful under that harsh gaze, then finally bent her head and turned her whole attention to her meal.

Even though Kane had deflected Ramona's attack, Rio's frail confidence had taken a blow. No doubt there were many other people who'd be at the visitation tonight and the funeral tomorrow who would think those same things.

The reminder added nervousness to the grief she already felt, and all but demolished her weak appetite. She forced herself to eat a few bites of steak, then made a try at the chocolate parfait Ardis brought in before she gave up. It was a huge relief to excuse herself from the table and retreat to her room.

* * *

The visitation at the funeral chapel in town was just as nerve-racking as Rio feared, but the worst part was bearing up under the ordeal of seeing Sam in his casket. The crushing grief she'd worked so hard to escape that day overwhelmed her, leaving her raw emotions more battered than ever.

Ramona added her touch to the cheerless evening, doing everything she could to ensure that she and Tracy were all but attached to Kane's arms. It looked to Rio as if Kane and Ramona had smoothed over their differences. Certainly no outsider could have detected anything but closeness between the three, because Rio could not.

She stood carefully to the side, a bit away from the threesome so she wouldn't look presumptuous. She lost count of the number of people who eventually got around to her and asked what her plans were now that Sam had passed on.

She did her best to evade the question when she could, until her raw emotions and bad nerves became too much. She was about to slip away when the soft chime of the clock in the foyer of the funeral chapel marked the hour.

It wasn't long after that before the suffocating crowd began to ebb away, taking much of Rio's tension with it. To her vast relief, Ramona and Tracy walked out with the last cluster of people, until only she and Kane remained.

By the time they reached Kane's car, the sun had set and most of the traffic had thinned. Kane opened her door for her, then closed it solidly beside her once she was inside.

The black dress she'd chosen for tonight was less formal than the one she planned to wear for the funeral. Less formal and with a shorter hem, she was reminded as she again tried to adjust the slim skirt so it didn't reveal so much of her legs. She'd just got settled when Kane got behind the wheel and shoved his key into the ignition. The expensive car purred to life, but he didn't immediately put it into gear.

He was wearing one of his best suits, the fine cut and black color emphasizing his size and his very masculine physique. By comparison, with her hair up, the black dress on and the slinky feel of silk stockings and satiny underthings, Rio felt supremely feminine.

Guilt assailed her for the thoughts that had nothing to do with grief. She felt her face pale and turned her head to stare miserably out her window. She jumped when Kane touched her wrist.

"Are you all right?" Kane's voice was a low, warm drawl, and Rio swore she could feel it gust gently across her skin. His strong, calloused fingers slid down her wrist to her hand. Rio turned her head and looked at him before her gaze fled the calm watchfulness in his.

His hand wrapped around hers and the firm flex of his fingers pressed her palm against the hardness of his. Rio cautiously forced her gaze back to his, as fearful as she was amazed that he was touching her like this. The bleakness in his blue eyes matched hers, and she realized that the small gesture was an acknowledgment, however fleeting, of their common grief.

"Are you all right?" she returned quietly. "I don't think I told you that I'm sorry your father—"

She'd been doing so well that her sudden inability to finish what she'd meant to say surprised her. Kane's grip tightened briefly.

"I know."

With that, Kane slowly let go of her hand and faced forward a few moments. She was watching when his expression hardened, when the grimness came back over him. He reached down to put the car into gear, then slowly pulled away from the curb.

The other business that he'd mentioned to Ramona didn't materialize. The long ride home through the dark, star-studded night was slow and silent.

Rio slept poorly that night. She awoke feeling heavy-hearted. The 5:00 a.m. breakfast she was accustomed to had been delayed until seven, so Ramona and Tracy could join them and Ardis would be spared having to prepare two meals. She was so restless by the time she dressed in slacks and a blouse to go downstairs that her insides were in knots.

The moment she got to the hall outside the dining room, she heard Ramona's voice. "All right, Kane, perhaps I *should* explain why I despise Rio Cory."

Rio came to an abrupt halt in the hall. Indecision made her take a half step back before Ramona's next words froze her.

"I don't think her relationship with your father was healthy at all. Not that Sam, rest his dear soul, ever did anything dishonorable," she hastily added. "But God knows how it's looked to everyone else with her hanging around all these years, fawning over him. I'm ashamed to say that several people have made remarks to me about her.''

Kane said something to Ramona then, but his voice was so low that Rio couldn't make out the words.

A second later Ramona blurted, ''Dear Lord, that girl came between Sam and I from the beginning! She made me feel as if I didn't belong here, as if I was too citified and frivolous to bother with. And she was so unkind to poor little Tracy—oh, not in front of the two of you, she was too clever for that—but in secret. Tracy came crying to me many times, heartbroken and mystified by Rio's jealousy and spitefulness. If Sam hadn't felt so sorry for her, the four of us might have had a happy little family...Sam and I might have had a different marriage.''

Ramona's voice broke tragically on the word before she paused, then continued in a voice sharp with dislike. ''But it's too late now, too late because of *her*. And if losing my dear sweet Sam isn't bad enough, then it's the worry that she's still so obsessed with him that she'll cause a huge scene at the funeral. My God, we'll be lucky if she doesn't throw herself on the casket and beg to be buried with him! Oh, Kane, what can we do? That girl has robbed us all of so much!''

The tide of nausea and outrage that swept Rio made her step back, staggered by the monstrousness of what she'd just heard. She was shaking so badly that as she turned to retreat to her room, her knees almost gave way.

The added shock of suddenly coming face-to-face

with Tracy, who must have been standing just behind her, almost accomplished what her mother's cruel words had started. Tiny dark spots swirled before her eyes and she felt her body start to go limp for a terrifying second before she somehow rallied and stayed upright.

Tracy stared at her a moment, then looked away. The aloof set of her delicate profile gave Rio the impression that she'd heard the outlandish things her mother had said. That she didn't intend to get involved—even if it meant condoning a pack of lies—was clear by her tight-lipped silence.

Tracy's complete lack of friendliness toward her had been perplexing, but there was no way now to avoid the notion that Tracy had turned against her. Since she and Tracy had gotten along well in the past, she couldn't begin to guess the reason.

Rio stepped around her and retreated to her room in a haze of fresh shock.

For someone who shrank from emotional displays, Rio's worry that the rising tide of grief she felt would overwhelm her self-control added a new torment to the painful business of the day. Of the cruel things Ramona had said that morning, the one that haunted Rio was the remark about throwing herself on the casket.

With the funeral a mere hour away, the volatile mixture of heartbreak and nerves combined with the terror of being completely alone in the world. The knowledge that there was a tiny, sad part of her that almost wished she could be buried with Sam only magnified the horrid possibilities that Ramona's cruel words had conjured up.

Though she would never do anything as dramatic as throw herself on Sam's casket, the notion that she might be capable of making a scene that would shame her—or worse, shame Sam—upset her deeply. Later, when she tried to brush her hair and pin the hip-length tresses into a conservative knot, she was shaking. Again and again, the thick length escaped confinement before she could get it pinned into place.

By the time a knock came at the door, her hair still wasn't tamed and she hadn't even tried to put on her dress. Holding on to the thick swath of dark hair, she hurried to the door, certain it was Ardis or Estelle reminding her of the time.

She pulled the door open, saw it was Kane, then shoved the door closed until it was only open a crack. Her cheeks burned at the knowledge that Kane had seen her in little more than her black slip and stockings.

"Are you about ready?" The gruff words sounded impatient.

Rio glanced over her shoulder, spied the black dress on the bed, then was suddenly, maddeningly overcome with emotion. The knowledge that she was too upset to get ready in a timely manner undermined her confidence in being able to handle herself at the funeral. Oh, God, she couldn't go disheveled, and she couldn't go if she was going to burst into tears and weep through the service.

She'd lived her whole life under the scrutiny of a community that had more bad expectations of her than good. Because she didn't want to bring scorn on Sam's faith in her, there was no way she could appear before these people and be anything short of perfectly groomed, perfectly behaved. And if she couldn't...

"Go on ahead, Kane," she called softly. "I'll be along later."

His low, "What?" was terse.

"I can drive myself," she offered in a more confident voice, then gasped and jumped back when her door swung sharply inward.

"We go together," he growled.

"But I'm not ready—my hair," she said, feeling again the precariousness of her control.

The sudden realization that Kane's blue gaze was sliding slowly over the curves accentuated by her black slip made her breath catch. Flustered, she let her hair swing loose and she turned from him. The door closed behind her with a quiet click. She glanced back, relieved until she saw that Kane hadn't gone.

"Just run a brush through it," he told her, then nodded toward the dress on the bed. "That what you're wearing?" He walked over and picked up the dress in one large hand, then turned back to her and held it out.

The sheer forcefulness of the gesture underscored his determination to rush her. It was also a signal to her that the perfect appearance, perfect behavior she was worried sick over meant nothing to him. As she meant nothing to him.

She turned from him suddenly, then hurried to the mirror over her vanity table. A few quick strokes of the brush and her hair was again tidy enough to put up. She managed to gather it and twist it over and over until she'd wound it into a thick knot.

With fingers that had somehow lost their dexterity, she tried to shove enough hairpins into place to hold the knot just so. Seconds after she'd finished, it all began to unravel.

"Go on without me," she snapped, so frustrated that she began tearing at the hairpins.

Kane's abrupt move—which sent her dress sailing back onto the bed—drew her attention to his reflection in the vanity mirror. He stalked toward her, then to her complete surprise, he reached past her and grabbed up the brush.

The moment he gathered her hair in his big hand, she felt prickles of sensation strike her scalp like tiny lightning bolts. She tensed, expecting him to yank the brush through the dark tresses as mercilessly as she had earlier, but the brush strokes that began near the ends of her hair were brisk, gentle. As he worked his way up the length to the top of her head, he efficiently banished the tangles, until he was merely brushing her hair, running the brush from the crown of her head to the blunt-cut ends.

Rio stood, nearly paralyzed by surge after surge of pleasure as Kane wielded the brush. Her eyes were riveted to his reflection in the mirror, fascinated by the absorption on his harsh, handsome face.

Everything slowed in those quiet moments. The whisper of the brush marked the time that passed. At last his gaze lifted and met hers in the mirror. The brush made one last pass that was slower than the rest before it reached the end of its path and fell away.

"What's wrong with wearing it loose?" he asked, his voice a quiet rasp.

His question dispelled the peculiar lethargy that had gripped her. The answer brought a swift sting of tears. "Because I need to look conservative," she managed to tell him.

Kane's lips quirked with disbelief. "Conservative? What the hell for?"

She could barely get out the words. "For Sam." Honesty made her add, "And because someone might disapprove."

"Of what? Wearing your hair down?" He looked incredulous.

"You wouldn't understand," she said quietly as she broke eye contact with his reflection. She turned toward him to take her brush.

"Try me." The terse words were a demand. When he didn't release the brush, she glanced up at him momentarily, then away.

"Please, Kane," she whispered, but her small tug on the brush only made him tighten his grip. She took in an uneven breath. "You know how people feel about me."

"How's that?"

Rio felt such a surge of hurt that she almost couldn't get the words out. "Don't pretend you don't know." She made herself look at him as she said, "No one's more critical of me than you—unless it's Ramona."

Kane's expression went stiff. Rio tried again to take her brush, but Kane glanced past her, saw her handbag on the vanity top and reached for it. Just that quickly, he'd shoved the brush into the purse, hesitated, then pinched a wad of tissues from the nearby dispenser and crammed them in, too.   His, "Get the dress on," was low and angry as he fumbled with the zipper and flap on the purse.

Rio stared at his harsh profile as a fresh tide of sadness rose in her heart. Wordlessly, she walked to the bed, picked up the dress, then tugged it over her head and smoothed it down.

Remorse stole over her. Kane's father had died, and she was more worried over how she wore her hair than being ready for the funeral on time. She got out a quiet, "I'm sorry, Kane. I don't mean to cause problems," as she pulled her hair forward, then reached behind her back and tried to slide the zipper up.

To her surprise, Kane's fingers brushed hers aside. He slid the zipper up in no time, and Rio pushed her hair back over her shoulder to let it stream down her back.

The next thing she knew, Kane stepped so close to her that she felt the heat that radiated from his tall, strong body. Her breath stopped as his hands slid around her waist to pull her back against him. Her soft sound of surprise and her self-conscious move to step away made him tighten his arms and lower his head to press his jaw against her cheek.

The heat that scorched through their clothes enveloped her in weakness. She could feel every detail of his unyielding maleness, and something deep and primitive and female in her stirred.

She rested her hands hesitantly on the thick-muscled forearms that were cinched around her. Kane rubbed his jaw against her soft skin, and drew her even closer to him.

Oh, God, it was heaven to stand there like that! Heaven to feel his arms around her, his body against hers, heaven to feel the physical comfort he was lavishing on her, whether he knew it or not. Whether he meant to or not.

The sharp edge of feminine arousal that followed shocked her. She couldn't help that she'd raised her hand to gently place her palm along his strong jaw. The freshly shaved skin was softer than she'd expected and she couldn't resist exploring the smooth texture with her fingertips.

Suddenly she felt ashamed of herself, ashamed to be standing there with Kane, practically trembling with longing and desire. They were burying Sam today. She had no business feeling anything but grief. Misery came roaring back, worse than ever.

She slid her hand from Kane's jaw, then turned abruptly, stepping neatly out of his arms before she stopped, her face turned slightly away from him. She reached for the handbag Kane had tossed to the bed, rummaged nervously for the brush, then ran it briskly through her hair to smooth it a last time.

When she finished, the room was utterly still. She didn't need to see or hear him to know that Kane was there, silently watching her, because she felt his long, unhurried scrutiny as if he were running his hands over her.

"You're beautiful." The rasped words were an accusation, but his next ones softened it. "Anyone who can criticize the way you look, especially right now, can go straight to hell.''

His gruff fervency brought such a sharp sting of tears that a couple spurted down her cheek before she could control them. She dashed them away with her hand, striving to make the gesture look as natural as possible. She couldn't look at him and her soft, ''Thanks,'' was choked. She put the brush away and closed her purse. ''I'm ready.''

The small declaration was a lie. She wasn't ready for this final goodbye to Sam, but admitted to herself that she might never be. As she started toward the door, her legs seemed to grow more heavy with each step.

She and Kane left her room and went downstairs without speaking. At a quick word from Kane, Rio waited in the front hall near the door while he stepped into the living room to let Ramona and Tracy know they were ready to leave.

She heard Ramona say something then abruptly cut herself off. Rio pretended not to notice that the older woman was flushed with temper when they all joined her. Kane opened the door, ushering Tracy and Ramona through it before he held his hand out to Rio.

Assuming he was hurrying her along, Rio stepped past him and followed the other two women. Kane caught her arm, then tugged her to a halt while he closed the door behind them. His hand was wrapped around hers as they walked to the waiting limousine. No one was more surprised than Rio when Kane sat next to her, his strong arm on the seat behind her shoulders in a gesture as possessive as it was protective.

CHAPTER SIX

THE funeral took place in the country church Sam had faithfully attended since childhood. The graveside service was held at the Painted Fence just before noon.

Rio was grateful for Kane's constant presence at her side. At first, she'd felt wooden with him, unaccustomed to being touched by him—by anyone—in public. The fact that every eye strayed their way often enough to catch Kane touch her arm or take her hand only compounded her unease. But once the funeral started, the battle to keep her emotions under severe control made her forget everything but getting through the somber service.

The eulogy made her cry, ruining her intention to remain dry-eyed. The service came to a close at last, with the mourners filing quietly out while family remained seated.

When it was time for the four of them to go out to the limousine that would follow the hearse to Langtry and the gravesite, Kane again took her arm, allowing Ramona and Tracy to precede them.

None of them spoke during the ride to the ranch. Ramona sat as still and perfect as cool porcelain, while Tracy tried to powder the redness from around her eyes. Kane sat between Rio and the door, his arm again resting over the back of the seat behind her.

When they turned off the highway onto the ranch

road, then finally onto the much rougher twin tracks that led to the private graveyard, Rio's heart grew heavier than ever. The royal blue awning pitched over the open grave was colorful enough to hurt the eyes in the bright sun. Rio couldn't look as the hearse came to a halt and the pallbearers removed the casket to carry it to the grave.

Kane handed Rio out of the car. He hung back to assist Tracy, then Ramona who had spurned the funeral director's effort to help her out the other side. Ramona latched onto Kane's arm, discreetly snapped her fingers in a silent order for Tracy to take his other arm, then stepped forward regally, sweeping them past Rio and leaving her to follow alone. Clearly, Kane had become the prize in the war Ramona seemed intent upon waging.

The huge chain of cars and pickups that had followed in the funeral procession across Langtry range were pulling up. The long line of vehicles broke gradually, parking in shorter rows around the fenced cemetery so no one would have to walk far. Rio followed the other three, surprised when, before Kane had taken another half dozen steps, he had tactfully disengaged himself from both Ramona and Tracy.

Rio could see Ramona fairly vibrate with outrage as Kane gently pressed her and Tracy forward while he hung back. Tracy meekly touched her mother's arm only to find her shy touch thrown off as Ramona marched on indignantly. Kane turned toward Rio and waited until she caught up to him.

Rio couldn't meet Kane's eyes as she joined him and they walked together toward the cemetery. She couldn't let him see that for one bright exhilarating moment on that dark, sad day, that her foolish heart was thrilled by his attention, and almost giddy with speculation about what it all meant.

Those few seconds of brightness dulled as they walked through the open gate toward the blue awning. Ramona and Tracy had already been seated across from the casket. Funeral attendants were still racing back and forth bringing more flowers, though most of them were already being sent to nursing homes and hospitals in the area. The minister was taking his place next to the casket, leafing through his prayer book.

The Langtry ranch hands had shown up, most in their best finery. Boz was one who stood just outside the whitewashed fence near the head of the casket and Rio walked over to grip the old cowboy's hand. The men next to Boz nodded to her in deference or took her hand for a brief handshake. Kane had followed Rio and was himself shaking hands and receiving quiet words of condolence.

When they finished, Kane escorted her back to the row of chairs across from the casket. He seated her next to Tracy, then ignored the chair set out for him as he stood behind the two of them.

The graveside service was brief. The procession of mourners who filed past them to shake hands or express condolences seemed endless in the noontime heat. In the end, it was the heat that prompted Kane to interrupt the procession early and suggest that they all head to the house where it was cool and lunch would be served.

It was a relief to be able to retreat to the limousine

that had been left idling with the air conditioner running. The moment the door was closed behind them and the tinted glass obscured the inside of the limo, Ramona's lovely face turned petulant. Not a hint of tears marred her perfectly made-up features, though Rio noted the woman had a lace hankie at the ready.

With a selfish lack of concern for Kane's grief, Ramona turned toward him, a militant expression on her face. "Why on earth is Sam being buried next to that—that Cory woman?" After all these years, the shock of hearing anyone refer to her late mother as "that Cory woman" jarred her. A brief flash of memory—the tall dark-haired woman with the musical voice and the gentle touch—burst through her grief for Sam, compounding it somehow and bringing a fresh rush of tears.

The second shock Rio suffered was when she realized that Sam was indeed about to be buried next to her mother. She glanced toward the cemetery in a fog of disbelief as she belatedly acknowledged that she'd been so intent on the service that she'd failed to notice how close Sam's grave was to her mother's. Their graves couldn't have been much closer, particularly in that part of the cemetery where the only graves would be theirs.

"My God, Kane," Ramona was saying, her voice trembling, "you've got to tell them to dig a new grave—away from *there!*"

"My father's instructions were precise." Kane's harsh tone was final.

Rio glanced toward Kane, unable to conceal her surprise. Sam had instructed Kane to bury him that close to her mother? The fact that Sam had wanted it done and that Kane had done it—in the face of his dislike for the Cory's and the speculation and gossip such a thing was sure to cause—astonished her.

"I don't understand..." The words were barely out of her mouth before Kane's eyes shifted and bore down sharply into hers. The impact of his glittering blue gaze silenced her and Rio faced forward, her mind spinning as she searched her memories of her mother—and her memories of Sam—for something that would explain Sam's stunning order.

Rio had known Sam to at times become strangely gruff when they'd talked about Lenore Cory. She'd always suspected he'd had some special feelings for her mother, but to leave instructions that he be buried next to her indicated something much more significant than casual admiration.

The whole idea made her feel strange, as if there was some enormous secret that she'd been too dull-witted to sense. As the limo pulled forward slowly and rolled into a wide turn that would take it back down the twin tracks, Rio glanced toward the blue awning. Again she saw the close proximity of the two graves and felt another little start of surprise.

Fortunately, Ramona said no more, though the silence from her end of the long seat was turbulent. The tension between the four of them was so pronounced that Rio couldn't wait to arrive back at the ranch house. Once there, Kane got out of the limo and turned to hold the door for her. Rio got out hastily and walked quickly to the ranch house.

There had to be two hundred people in the house

and on the patio behind, with more people walking from parked cars. Kane had hired caterers to provide a buffet, and they had set up in the formal dining room. A double line of guests was filing through the dining room, then exiting toward the patio or one of the other rooms on the main floor.

To Rio, it was a nightmare. People were everywhere. The strain of the day was telling on her, making her feel light-headed. She'd lost track of where Kane was, and made her way through the front hall, finding herself waylaid several times by ranching neighbors and business associates of Sam's and Kane's.

Suddenly, Ty Cameron, the rancher who'd sold Kane the bull, stepped into her path. Tall and handsome, his blond hair a bright mix of bronze and wheat and white from the sun, Ty was ruggedly handsome and was what Rio thought of as cowboy gallant.

"Hello, Miz Rio," he said, his deep drawl somber. "I'm real sorry about Sam. I know the two of you were close."

Rio managed a tight smile and nodded her thanks.

"I was about to find myself something cool to drink. Can I get you something?" Ty gently took her arm and tugged her a little more out of the current of passing guests before he released her.

"I—I was thinking of that myself," she managed, a faint hint of color seeping into her cheeks. Ty's eyes were a warm, gold-flecked blue, and the intensity in them as they roamed her face made Rio feel self-conscious. His eyes crinkled at the corners when he smiled down at her.

"If you'll allow me, Miz Rio," he said, his voice charmingly formal, "I'd like to escort you someplace where you can sit down awhile. I can get whatever you want to drink on ice and bring it to you quick."

Rio glanced away momentarily, and felt the color in her cheeks rise higher. "That's very nice of you, Mr. Cameron, but you must be hungry. Why don't we get something in the dining room?"

Ty led the way with his hand solicitously around her elbow, keeping her slightly behind him as he made a path through the crowd. It amazed her how quickly he managed to get them to the buffet table. Though Rio had no appetite, she made a few selections, mindful of her increasing light-headedness and the fact that she hadn't eaten since the day before.

They left the dining room carrying their drinks and plates. Every available seat was taken in the house. They walked to the kitchen, and Rio came to a halt as she glanced through the door to the patio and saw that every seat available in the shade outside was occupied, as well.

She turned to Ty. "It looks like it's no better outside. If you don't mind, we might find a place to sit on the stairs."

"The stairs would be fine," he returned, then let her lead the way to the staircase that opened off the back hall. Rio sat down on the third step from the bottom. Ty sat beside her.

Though she was initially stiff with the handsome rancher, she gradually relaxed. They talked about ranching, but Ty didn't ask her what her plans were now, as nearly everyone else had. It seemed he was the only person in Texas who didn't assume Kane would never let her stay on.

On the other hand, there was something speculative in his gaze, something that suggested he had made the same assumptions as everyone else, but was too much a gentleman to let on.

His solicitous, "I'd be happy to get you something more to eat or another glass of tea, Miz Rio," prompted her to shake her head.

"Thank you, no, but go ahead if you'd like something," she told him.

"I'm full enough for a hot day," he said, then reached over to relieve her of her plate and sit it with his on a step behind them. When he turned back, his eyes made a brisk search of her face.

"My ranch manager is buying a ranch of his own, so I'm looking for someone with experience running a place the size of Cameron." He gave her a half smile that was loaded with masculine appeal. "I thought I'd mention it to you in case you ever got the notion to try a new challenge."

As he spoke, he slipped a hand to the inside pocket of his suit jacket. He withdrew a business card and passed it to her. "If I'm not available at that number, my people will have instructions to notify me immediately of your call, and I'll get back to you right away." He shrugged. "Or, if you'd just like to get away sometime, I'd be honored to take you to dinner and show you what we do for excitement down in San Antone." The smile he gave her was warm, and there was no mistaking the personal interest in the gaze that was fixed so intently on her face.

Rio glanced down at the card. The possible offer of a job as good as this made her feel less terrified of the future, but the personal offer made her wary. She hoped her soft, "Thank you, Mr. Cameron, we'll see," as she lifted her gaze to meet his would be taken as a more businesslike response than a personal one.

On the other hand, what would it hurt if things did get personal between them? As she considered what she knew of Ty Cameron's character along with his rugged good looks, she realized he was probably the only man she'd ever met who had the potential to make her fall for him and forget her feelings for Kane.

As if the possibility of caring for someone else and forgetting her feelings for Kane was destined to be thwarted, she heard a sound, then turned her head to see Kane standing next to the staircase. His blue gaze shifted from her face to Ty's before it shot back to hers and narrowed.

"There are people asking after you," he said gruffly, managing to make her feel in the wrong.

Ty said smoothly, "That's my fault, I'm afraid. I've been dominating Miz Rio's time." Ty got to his feet, then reached out to shake Kane's hand and offer condolences.

Rio stood to her feet while the two men talked briefly, stepping out of the way when a waiter came scurrying down the hall to collect their empty plates and glasses. Kane seemed to relax a bit as he returned the handshake, but by the time Ty had taken his leave of them both, his expression was again stony with disapproval.

"Is there a reason the two of you were hiding out back here?"

Kane's terse question took her aback. She answered before she thought about it. "There was no other place to sit."

"Some rental place called," he went on irritably, as if her answer was too trivial to acknowledge. No doubt he was annoyed at being bothered by the call. "They wanted to let you know the trailer you reserved is ready. I told them to hold it another day."

Rio shook her head slightly. "I need it today."

"Not with a crowd around to watch the little melodrama of Rio Cory packing her things and driving off into the great unknown," he said grimly.

The words stung. It was as if those few moments of closeness they'd experienced that day hadn't happened. Rio turned from him and walked briskly toward the front of the huge home. The grief that had seemed to ease the past half hour settled back into place, bringing with it a fresh sense of loneliness.

Rio made her way through the crowd, stopping to speak briefly here and there, doing her best to be as visible as possible for as long as she could stand before she slipped away to the quiet of her room.

She never had an opportunity to leave the ranch that day after all. Guests came and went at the main house until after seven that evening. Two of Kane's cousins from his mother's side of the family stayed the night, not leaving the ranch until late afternoon the next day.

Too restless to wait around at the house, Rio put in a full day's work so Kane could visit with his cousins.

By the time she got to the house that evening, she felt uncommonly tired, and didn't care if she ate supper or not. The fact that Ramona would be at the table was added incentive to forgo the meal.

Rio stopped in the kitchen only long enough to grab a small jar of fruit juice from the refrigerator and tell Ardis not to set a place for her. She went upstairs to her room, her feet so leaden with fatigue that she almost wished she'd taken Sam's elevator.

The emptiness she'd run from that whole day was suddenly so much worse in the silence of the big house. Ardis had given her usual taciturn greeting of "Evenin'," but Sam wasn't somewhere nearby calling out to her or asking about her day.

Rio stepped into her room and closed the door, then walked across the floor to her private bath. It seemed to take forever to get her clothes off, unbraid her hair and step beneath the hot spray of the shower.

When she stepped out later, wound her hair in a huge towel and dried off, she felt more exhausted than ever. Finishing the fruit juice refreshed her a bit, but by the time she'd wrapped up in a robe, brushed her teeth and dried her hair, she was worn out.

She walked into her bedroom, and was about to turn down the comforter and top sheet when she was startled by a knock at the door. She cinched the belt of her robe tighter and was halfway to the door when the knock came again, louder. Kane called out an irritable, "Where the hell are you, Rio?"

Rio opened the door a few inches and looked out at Kane's dark expression. "Where do you think?"

she answered in a false show of spirit, secretly hurt by his impatience.

"We're waiting supper for you," he said gruffly.

"I told Ardis—"

"I know what you told Ardis," he cut in. "Get dressed and come down anyway."

A flash of temper banished some of Rio's fatigue. "My workday's over," she told him. "Permanently. Find someone else to boss around." She gave the door a smart shove to close it in his arrogant face when his hand flew up to stop it.

The look in his eyes was dangerously grim. He walked forward slowly, his hand on the edge of the door to push it wide. Rio stepped back.

"I'm asking you to get dressed and come down to supper," he said in a low, rough voice.

Rio's chin came up. "And I'm telling you that I'm going to bed now. I could care less about eating."

"Are you sick?"

She must have been imagining the hint of concern in his eyes. She shook her head. "Just tired. I'm not up to you and Ramona tonight." She gave him a humorless quirk of lips. "No offense."

Kane's stiff smile was just as humorless. He stepped farther into the room and closed the door. "What are your plans for tomorrow?"

"To leave Langtry," she answered simply, drawing herself up a bit straighter as she said it. Not for anything did she want Kane to see how much it hurt to have to leave her home. If things had been different between them, she might have moved out of the main house into the quarters at the end of the bunk house.

She loved the ranch, loved the outdoor work, and would have been content to stay on indefinitely as a ranch hand. Because of Kane, she couldn't.

"The lawyer's coming out tomorrow morning. He'll be reading the will," he said. It was clear by his low, rough voice that he wasn't happy to have to tell her anything about it. His brusque, "I understand from him that you need to be present," explained why.

Rio shook her head. "The will doesn't concern me. The only thing I'm interested in is the letter Sam mentioned that day." She'd been unable to forget Sam's weak, *Letters say for me,* as he lay dying. If he really had left a letter for her, it would be like one last talk, a keepsake she could see and touch and take with her.

"The lawyer mentioned he had them. He'll pass them out after the will is read."

Rio turned away, wearily shaking her head. "I'm only interested in Sam's letter." She brushed a wide swath of hair behind her shoulder and walked to her bed to tug the comforter and sheet down. She lifted her hands to the belt on her robe and paused. "Could you please close the door on your way out?"

She stood there for several long moments. There was no sound from Kane, not even a whisper of movement. Finally, she glanced back, saw Kane's dark expression, then felt herself wilt a little more. "Please take your angry looks someplace else, Kane," she said softly as she faced forward.

The sound of Kane walking up behind her made her stiffen. The big hands that settled over her shoulders were warm and sure, and Rio tried to move away from him. Kane thwarted her with the tight flex of his strong fingers.

"Just stand still," he whispered gruffly. His right hand lifted from her shoulder. "You've got something in your hair. Looks like a pillow feather." She felt him comb his fingers down the length of her hair, sending a shower of bright sensations across her skin from her scalp to her toes. Her legs began to weaken as heat flooded her. Kane lifted his hand to run his fingers down her hair a second time and she twisted abruptly from him.

The grip he had on her other shoulder when she wrenched away pulled her robe open. Kane caught her wrist with an ease that mocked her quick move, and his blue gaze dropped to the shoulder and breast that had been uncovered. Rio grabbed for the edge of her robe to cover herself, but he seized her other wrist.

His eyes fixed on her bare breast and darkened. Her gasp drew his attention to her mouth for a fraction of a second before his gaze fell again to her exposed flesh.

Rio realized dazedly that he was drawing her closer, and tried to pull away from him. Though years of ranch work had made her strong, she was no match for Kane's superior strength. Their brief struggle managed only to loosen the tie belt until the top of the robe gaped open.

She froze, her cheeks flushing a dark red. In the next instant Kane released her wrists and slid his calloused hands around her bare waist. She grabbed for the edges of her robe to close it, but the hot, determined look in his eyes made her fingers sluggish. She stared up at him, mesmerized as his lips descended to hers.

The next thing she knew, she was lying back on her bed, pressed to the mattress by Kane's big body. His denim-clad leg slid between hers and more of his weight shifted atop her until he was lying fully on her, his clothing gently abrading her tender skin. And all the while he was kissing her, dominating her with the skill of his lips and tongue and hands until she wept with frustration at her body's helpless response.

Suddenly his mouth slid off hers and he dropped his forehead to the mattress beside her head. The low growl that rumbled up from his chest was shockingly feral and sent a light shiver of fear through her.

"Damn it," he growled, then turned his head until his lips were touching the shell of her ear. "What is it about you?" he demanded softly. "If I take you here, right now," he said as his hand found the soft mound of her breast and toyed aggressively with its tip, "then maybe you can get the hell off Langtry and I'll never give you another thought."

The words were unbearably cruel, but the tender expertise of his fingers made her move restlessly beneath him. The terrible confusion of cruelty and sharp pleasure tore at her. A silent sob rose painfully in her chest, but she bit her lip until she tasted blood to stifle it.

"I hate wanting you," he growled. "I hate looking at you and knowing that you're not only the one woman I ache to have, but the last one I want."

The breath she'd been holding gusted out on a wave of pure misery. She turned her face away. Her voice was so hoarse that it was barely audible. "Rio Cory, tomboy trash, daddy caused an awful crash. Killed them two boys, killed himself, now he's gone to drunkard's hell."

The silence that descended was thunderous. Rio's blood was pounding in her ears. She'd never repeated to anyone, not even Sam, the malicious little verse she'd been tortured with those years after her father's death. The mayor's daughter was the first to actually say it in her presence, but it had been rapidly picked up by her classmates. It had seemed to take forever for everyone to forget the awful rhyme.

But nobody forgot, not really. She was still "that Cory girl" no matter what she'd done, no matter what Sam had tried to do for her. Wasn't Kane's insulting declaration proof of that?

Heartache and exhaustion took the last of her strength. She let her hands slide from his wide shoulders. She all but wilted beneath the warm crush of his hard body, her face turned away, tears leaking from her eyes.

"I hate wanting you, too, Kane," she whispered. "I'm ashamed that I've loved someone all these years who holds me in such contempt."

At last Kane's fingers stopped toying with her breast. She shivered when he pulled the soft terry cloth of her robe over it. He slowly shifted himself off her, then quietly drew the facings of her robe together until they overlapped from neck to hem, covering her nakedness.

Rio was too exhausted and too dispirited to even open her eyes as she waited in the harsh silence for

Kane to move off the bed and leave the room. She felt him shift, then felt the warm gust of his breath the second before his lips touched her neck. His hand slid around her waist and pulled her tighter against him, but Rio didn't move.

"Oh, God, Rio, I must be losing my mind," he rasped as he nuzzled her neck, then drew back to smooth a few strands of hair from her temple. "Forgive me for being such a bastard."

Rio didn't answer. She couldn't. The weight of grief and disappointment pressed so heavily on her heart that she almost couldn't breathe. Kane eventually rolled away from her and got up. He must have taken her silence for sleep because he gently moved her until her head was on a pillow. He drew her robe more snugly around her and pulled the sheet and comforter over her. The light switched off and she listened to his booted tread as he walked to the door and left the room.

CHAPTER SEVEN

KANE took somber note of Rio's empty chair at the table that next morning. He knew she was awake—he'd heard her moving around in her room. He knew she'd slept the night through, because he'd checked on her several times during the restless night he'd put in.

Just when he was about to give up on her, he heard her quiet footsteps on the front stairs. Rio was probably the only person he knew who could wear boots and walk quiet. Even her spurs, when she wore them, didn't rattle and chime. She had a way of moving that didn't demand attention, but it was that very grace and elegance that made her stand out.

Rio Cory, tomboy trash... The hateful rhyme made another pass through his mind before he ruthlessly silenced it. So many things about Rio suddenly made sense.

"I was wondering if you were going to come down this early."

Kane's voice had a deep, rusty sound at 5:00 a.m. Rio walked toward her place at the long dining room table and slipped onto her usual chair across from him. She didn't look him in the eye and she didn't speak. There was nothing to say. Besides, he'd merely made a comment.

All she had to do was get through the next few hours. The last thing she felt like doing was eating the steak and eggs breakfast Ardis was carrying in. The fact that she hadn't eaten since noon the day before was her only incentive to show up for this meal. She'd chosen to have breakfast when Kane did because she knew he'd allow her to eat in peace. Ramona wouldn't be so charitable.

The silence between them was oppressive. Rio ate mechanically, forcing herself to chew her food. The time or two she'd dared a glance at Kane, her gaze had collided with the laser intensity of his. Eventually the self-consciousness she felt made it impossible to eat. She set her fork down and plucked her napkin from her lap to toss it next to her plate.

"Where are you off to?" he asked as she stood.

Rio stepped aside and pushed her chair up to the table. "I have to finish packing," she said quietly, then turned to start for the door.

"There's no need to rush off."

Kane's deep voice made her hesitate. She looked at him, meeting his gaze full-on before she shook her head. "There's every need, Kane. Especially after last night."

Her soft words intensified the stillness of the big room. The deep blue of his eyes flickered a moment, then dulled, but he didn't look away. Instead, his gaze made a lightning tour from her face to her toes before it sped back up to meet her eyes.

"Suit yourself."

Irrational as it was, that was the moment Rio realized that she still hoped Kane would ask her to stay on. She'd helped run Langtry for years, with the authority to act for him on many occasions. She'd done a competent job, but Kane's bad feelings toward her were evidently too strong for him to even suggest it.

After last night, it was probably just as well. She didn't have the strength to deal with too many incidents like that one. She still longed for him to kiss her again, to touch her that aggressively, but those very longings seemed perverse in the light of how much he disliked her.

Rio turned from him then and hurried upstairs to finish getting her things together.

Rio stood just inside the door of the den, as far out of the way as possible as Ramona and Tracy got settled on the sofa. Kane was standing in front of the massive bookcase that took up an entire wall, leaning back against it with his arms crossed over his wide chest.

The lawyer sat at the desk. In front of him was Sam Langtry's will and four copies laid out in a row along the front edge of the desk. He'd set a white envelope on top of each of the four copies. Though Rio couldn't read the words printed on the envelopes from where she stood, the lawyer had indicated there was an envelope addressed to each of them.

Rio tried not to fidget as the lawyer began reading the document. The solemnity of the occasion—the sheer formality of the legal phrases combined with the enormity of Sam Langtry's fortune—filled her with dread. As she listened to everything Sam had built and owned detailed and disbursed, the growing suspicion that Sam's affection for her might have prompted him to leave her something significant made her feel sick.

The first inheritance that meant anything was Ramona's. The clause the lawyer read reminded them all of the prenuptial agreement Sam and Ramona had signed. The fact that Sam had ruthlessly adhered to its limits was soon apparent. Ramona's gasp sounded abnormally loud in the quiet room, but the lawyer continued to read.

Tracy, however, fared spectacularly compared to her mother. From the sound of it, she'd never have to concern herself with money again.

Kane was next, inheriting the lion's share of everything Sam had owned. Aside from his several businesses and the various ranches Sam held title to in Texas, Langtry was the very last holding mentioned. The fact that Kane was due to inherit only half of Langtry gave the clue to what was coming.

As soon as Rio heard the words, "'I leave to my foster daughter, Rhea René Cory, known to all as Rio Cory...'" a wave of dizziness passed so forcefully over her that she felt faint.

"'...The sum of five million dollars...half interest in Langtry Ranch... Must remain a full and equal partner for a minimum of one year... After which time, she is free to do with her share of Langtry as she pleases, and she is entitled to all proceeds and profits thereof... Should she refuse to accept this inheritance, or refuse to adhere to the minimum time requirement of ownership set forth here, her half interest in Langtry Ranch will pass instead to the Texas chapter of Friends for Equal Rights for Animals.' ''

Rio sagged back against the wall, too stunned at the enormous bequest—and its bizarre consequence—to listen to the rest of what the lawyer read. When the lawyer finished, Rio glanced toward Kane, her heart falling at his stony expression. The blue gaze he turned her way glittered with an unholy mixture of anger and bitter humor.

"Friends for Equal Rights for Animals, huh?" Kane looked away from her and addressed the lawyer. "And I suppose that particular clause is ironclad."

It wasn't a question, but the lawyer nodded his head. Ramona was suddenly on her feet, shoving her way up the line of copies on the desk until she found the one with the envelope bearing her name. She snatched up both will and envelope, then marched from the room, her eyes fiery with hatred as they fixed on Rio those last seconds.

Tracy sat on the sofa, a dazed look on her face. The lawyer came around the desk and picked up a copy of the will with the envelope addressed to Tracy and handed it to her. He swiftly scooped up both Kane's and Rio's, stepping across to the door to hand Rio hers before he took Kane's to him.

Rio stared down at the envelope with her name on it in Sam's handwriting. She glanced up, her eyes going directly to Kane. Kane's face was more sober and stern than she'd ever seen it, and she felt her heart break a little. What had Sam done?

Too restless to remain in the room, Rio turned and

quickly left, rushing upstairs to the privacy of the bedroom that would remain hers for the next year.

Rio,
Since I don't know exactly how long I have left, I thought it best to put a few things in a letter to you, just in case I don't have the time or opportunity to say them at the end.

First off, one of the highlights of my life was when you came to live with us at the main house. You've been everything a man could want in a daughter: you're beautiful, smart, and you've got a gentle, loving heart. Your love and devotion to me, particularly these last years as my health was waning, is a source of comfort and great pride to me. As you are a source of comfort and great pride.

I'm sorry as I can be that you're hurting now, and that I'm the cause. It's not possible for me to spare you grief. It is possible for me to do what I can to be certain you always have a home and plenty in the way of material things. That's why I left you what I did. Giving you half of Langtry is the thing I most wanted to do for you at the end. I hope that when the year is up, you will retain your share of the ranch. It gives me great peace and satisfaction to know that you will be living on Langtry and that you will raise your children there.

You and Kane will likely have some troubles in the beginning, but I know the two of you will work things out. You're both smart people of good character and common sense, so, if nothing else, remember how much I loved you both and try a little harder to settle your differences. Somehow, I'll know when you do.

I've left a book for you—*Plant and Animal Species of the World*. It's not what the book is, but what it contains. Your beautiful mother once gave me a bouquet of flowers for my table that she'd grown herself. I pressed them in that book and kept them all these years. You'll find a few other keepsakes in those pages that will remind you of her. Forgive me for keeping them to myself all this time, but there never seemed to be a time when I wanted to part with them. They belong to you now.

Remember that I love you, my precious daughter. God bless you. May you have a good, long, healthy life and find more love and happiness than a body has a right to.

Love,
Sam

The letter made her cry. Rio lay on her bed in the silence of her room, in shock about what Sam had left her, and confused by further evidence of his deep affection for her mother.

She stayed in her room a long time, rereading Sam's letter, searching her memories of Sam and her mother as she tried to make sense of it all. Finally, she put the letter in the lacquered box she'd already packed. Since it was almost time for lunch, she stepped into her bath and splashed her face with cool water.

She hadn't expected to still be here for lunch. Normally, this was a workday, and she would have put in six hours of outside work by this time. Now that she wasn't leaving, it would seem even more a privilege to be able to come to the cool of the big house and eat in the quiet of the dining room.

The idea that for the next year she would be an equal partner with Kane in all this was staggering. The fact that she felt like a thief ensured that she would give back his family heritage on the very day the year was up.

Kane's and Ramona's reactions to the reading of the will made her apprehensive about going down for lunch. Only the reminder that she'd have to face them sometime made her start downstairs.

When Rio walked into the dining room, Kane and Tracy were sitting at the table. Tracy glanced at her, then away, but Kane's gaze followed her all the way to the table. Rio sat down at her usual spot and waited in painful suspense for Ardis to finish bringing in their food.

The silence between the three of them was daunting. At least Ramona didn't put in an appearance. Tracy finished her lunch, then excused herself to drive to town. Since this was the first meal in days that Rio had managed to eat most of, she did her best to clear her plate by the time Kane finished eating.

Kane leaned back in his chair, his hard eyes wandering over her face as he sipped his coffee. Rio brushed her lips with her napkin, unsure how to diffuse the anger she sensed in him.

She set the napkin aside and met his blue gaze directly. ''There are some things I'd like to talk about,'' she said quietly.

Kane's mouth slanted. "Same here. Where do we start?" The hint of sarcasm in his voice put her even more on edge.

"I can't keep the money or the half share of Langtry," she began. "I'll find a lawyer and start whatever legal action is needed to have it all transferred back to you—" Kane was shaking his head before she finished, so she asked, "Why not, then?"

"Because of the damned clause about that animal rights group," he said grimly.

"I know the clause makes it difficult, but I thought if I got a lawyer to draw up a private agreement to return it to you when the year is up, you'd know that I don't intend to keep it."

Kane's frown deepened. "Why would you do that?"

"Langtry is rightfully yours. The money shouldn't have gone to me, either. I know Sam meant well—"

Kane cut her off with a terse, "Scared of me?"

"Why would I be?" she asked, careful to hide her surprise at his perception.

"Because you're afraid it's going to be a year-long bronc-busting session between us if you don't." As if disgusted, he tossed his napkin to the table and stood up.

Rio got to her feet, too. "Will it be?"

Kane glared over at her, taking in the worry that ran so deep she couldn't quite conceal it from him. But then, he doubted she'd ever been able to conceal much from him. He'd always seen things in the beautiful blue of her eyes. The cruel rhyme made a lightning pass through his mind.

Suddenly what he saw was the fear of a lonely, tormented child who'd never valued riches or a fine home as much as she'd valued love and acceptance. There was no doubt in his mind that Rio Cory could give up a multimillion dollar inheritance without batting an eyelash if she thought it could buy even a token truce between them.

The whole idea made him angry. It also gave his heart a solid kick.

"We'll just have to see," he grumbled. He saw the quick drop of her gaze and sensed her dismay. His voice went lower. "You're free to go anywhere you want, do anything you want. If you want to turn down the inheritance before the year is up, go ahead. It would be the perfect revenge for you."

Rio's shocked gaze sped up to his and he went on. "I'm not about to promise you a year of peace and sweetness when we both know we're probably in for a choice piece of hell." He couldn't keep his gaze from making a slow, meaningful sweep of her very feminine body. "Stay or go, Rio. It's your choice. But don't stay thinking the two of us will ever be anything more to each other than we've ever been."

Rio couldn't say exactly why it hurt so much for Kane to remind her that her feelings for him were as futile as ever. Perhaps it was because he disliked her so much that he felt he had to pound the message home at every opportunity.

And perhaps he was right. Perhaps she was a fool who needed to be rebuffed and rejected until what she felt for him was crushed and killed. A great tide of exhaustion swept her. *Why had Sam done this?*

Rio somehow kept her voice steady as she pushed her chair up to the table. "I'd rather you ran Langtry. I can fill in when you need me to, as usual."

Kane was shaking his head again. "The will states that you have to stay on as a full and equal partner. Until we find out from the lawyer exactly what that means—"

"And who will guess that I'm not?"

"If you're staying, you're going to do exactly as the will requires. If you aren't, you might as well turn it all down now and get the hell off Langtry."

Rio felt her face flush. "Fine, but I don't want to live at the main house. The empty cottage by the pecan grove will do."

"Like hell it will," he groused. "You'll live in *this* house, just like you've always done, or you can haul your backside down the highway."

Rio was suddenly too furious to speak. Kane had never seemed more brutally domineering than he was at that moment. A secret part of her placed a high value on that dominance, but another part of her burned with the unfamiliar fire of pure rebellion.

Too upset to stay, she turned and stalked from the room.

The next several days were wearing. Rio asked Kane about the book Sam had left her. He didn't recall a book with that title, but he told her he'd keep an eye out for it. They were so busy making up for the time they'd lost to the funeral that it was soon evident that he'd forgotten about it. Rio searched the den herself, but there were no books with the title Sam had given her, not even in one of the cabinets.

Ramona and Tracy stayed on at the ranch, their presence adding to the friction between Rio and Kane. Rio didn't move out of the main house, and they were both forced to endure the discomfort of being nearly inseparable as Kane filled her in on more of the ranch's paperwork, legalities and tax information than she'd ever needed to know before.

He also outlined his short-range and long-range plans for Langtry, then told her gruffly that she had the right to either cooperate with those plans or to suggest others—for at least the next year. Rio had no intention of changing a thing. When she'd told him so, his angry glare had baffled her.

After a few days of having her outside work drastically curtailed, Rio grew restless. She and Kane were in the den one morning. He was showing her the new software he'd bought for their computer, when her gaze once again wandered toward the huge picture window that looked out on a section of the lawn and the ranch buildings beyond the wide driveway.

"Damn it, if you don't pay attention, we aren't going to get through this before nightfall." Kane reached past her, and punched the key he'd just told her to push. His temper had been hair-trigger all morning, sending Rio's downcast emotions into a fresh slide. She'd had trouble concentrating the past week—much to her frustration and to Kane's. She needed to be outside in the fresh air doing something physical to clear her head and lift her spirits, but Kane had been dogged on the subject of teaching her everything he thought she needed to know.

She had tolerated his near tyranny because she understood he might be worried about fulfilling the requirements of Sam's will. But he was wearing her down, and their close proximity to each other did nothing to help ease the painful tension between the two of them.

"I need to get out of the house for a while," she said as she rolled the desk chair back and got to her feet.

"You need to master this program," he grumbled.

Rio shook her head. "Later. I want to work that colt before it gets too hot."

"We've got people to take care of that colt. You're the only one who can take care of this," he said as he tossed the software manual to the corner of the desk.

"I need a break, Kane."

His brusque, "Take it, then," made her feel as if she didn't deserve it.

The soft knock on the open door of the den distracted them. Tracy stood shyly in the doorway dressed in a chic silk shirt and designer jeans.

Kane glanced over at her, the stern set of his rugged features softening as he smiled at his stepsister. "Did you decide to take me up on that offer?"

Tracy's fair cheeks colored delicately. "If you have time now," she said shyly, then cast a quick glance toward Rio. "And if I'm not interrupting something important."

"Nothing that can't wait," Rio offered pleasantly.

She'd been trying to break the ice with Tracy for days in an attempt at friendliness. She started around the desk for the door to leave the other two in private, but Tracy behaved toward Rio as she had all week, virtually ignoring her.

Though it was a relief to make a quick escape, Rio couldn't miss the gentle, affectionate look on Kane's face or the pink-cheeked glow on Tracy's. Her low spirits sunk further as something that felt a whole lot like jealousy pricked her heart.

Kane gradually let up on her, allowing and even encouraging her to work outside as she preferred. He made a series of small business trips that took him away from the ranch for a day at a time, but he was usually home by evening. Rio was grateful he wasn't gone long, particularly since Ramona and Tracy were still around. She couldn't remember a time that their visit had lasted longer than a week, so their continued presence made her uneasy.

Meanwhile, her energy seemed to have deserted her. Since she'd been an early riser all her life, she was baffled by the sudden difficulty she had getting up in the morning. Fatigue made her drag around most of the day, but at night, sleep was long in coming. Her appetite didn't improve, and she couldn't seem to concentrate. Weariness and frustration made her irritable.

She missed Sam terribly. The grief she felt ebbed into a melancholy that seemed to sap what was left of her energy. The morning she overslept, she awoke more groggy and exhausted than ever. It was almost ten o'clock before she got dressed and hurried down the lane to the stables, her stomach twisting with horror and guilt at starting the day so late. She was halfway to the stable when she met Kane.

"I was just coming to get you." The impatience she sensed in him made her feel worse.

"I'm sorry. I must not have set my alarm clock." She couldn't maintain contact with the probing look he was giving her.

"It doesn't look like the extra sleep did much for you," he said bluntly.

The truth was, it hadn't. She still felt tired enough to sleep the day away, but she was too ashamed of this sudden weakness to admit it to Kane. "Gee, thanks," she murmured, then started around him. Kane caught her arm and stopped her.

"Are you feeling all right?" The gentle concern in his voice warmed her, but she steeled herself against it.

She nodded, but didn't look at him. He tugged her closer, the heat from his body penetrating her clothes. The feel of his fingers encircling her upper arm sent a sensual charge through her that was only magnified by his nearness. His grip tightened slightly.

"Did you eat?"

Rio tried not to show her surprise at his question. "All I wanted," she answered, giving her arm a slight tug to free herself. Kane's grip was firm.

"And, as usual, it probably wasn't much," he grumbled. "How long do you think you can go without getting enough food and rest?"

Rio didn't let herself mistake his concern for caring. And because she didn't, his questions irritated her.

"I'll eat when I get hungry and I'll try to go to sleep earlier at night. That enough for you?" Rio lifted her gaze and glared up at him, hating that nothing between them changed for the better, not really.

"It's enough," he said as he released her. "The cabins and cow camps still need to be checked for repairs and supplies. Pick someone to take care of it, unless you'd rather see to it yourself."

Rio edged away, putting a small space between them. "I'll work the colt first, then if you don't mind, I'll pack a bag and a cell phone and take care of it." She didn't need to add that Ramona would be delighted for her to absent herself from the main house for a couple of days. Tracy certainly wouldn't miss her and, truth to tell, Kane himself was probably eager for her to leave for a while. He seemed to be taking her ongoing presence on Langtry remarkably well compared to what she'd expected, but then, it had only been a couple of weeks since the will had been read.

"Handle it however you want." Kane's gaze probed hers a moment more before it wandered over her face. "I'll be at the house until after lunch."

Rio nodded, then turned to head down the path to the stable.

CHAPTER EIGHT

THE sorrel colt was an enthusiastic student, even-tempered, willing and intelligent, but his high-energy exuberance made him a handful. Rio worked him in the round pen the first half hour before she rode him through the gate and along one of the alleys that cut through the corrals toward the range.

The colt fairly pranced with excitement, then responded to her minor scolding and her firm hand on the reins by walking a bit more sedately as they passed through the last gate.

She kept the horse under tight control until she felt his excitement moderate. She rode him to one of the creeks, then into the water. He shuddered beneath her as the water rushed around his ankles, so she urged him to the middle where the creek was knee-high. She stroked his neck and murmured words of praise and encouragement, then had him walk in the water parallel to the bank. They stayed in the creek until the young horse calmed and she felt him relax. After a few moments more, she reined him toward the bank and rode him out of the water.

They rode on for two hours and the colt did well, quickly obeying her signals as she took him from one gait to the next and rode him in a huge zigzag pattern that led them past several hazards. The creek was the first of those, then a couple of windmills, and four oil pumping stations. They practiced going through a gate several times before the colt stood quietly for Rio to reach down to open and close it. The young horse's resistance to allowing her to close and latch the gate once they were through was the biggest problem.

Rio rode him to a pasture with cattle next, and moved a handful of cows and calves a small distance before she turned from that and started working with her rope. The colt shied the first few times she tried to lasso a fence post, but soon tolerated the throw of the rope.

Deciding the colt knew enough to begin doing some real work, she coiled her rope and tied it on her saddle before she started back for the headquarters. They took a different way back, again zigzagging to visit a few other hazards.

Working the colt on the range had lifted some of her gloom and caused her tiredness to ease, but the hollow feeling of sadness was as heavy as ever. Now that the colt was moving along, competently responding to her signals, her mind started to wander.

She thought about the book Sam had left her, and felt a new pang. She hadn't been able to find it in the den or in any of the other bookcases around the huge house. The only place she hadn't checked was Sam's room. She'd reminded Kane about it a couple of days before, but he'd evidently forgotten it again. Perhaps she should suggest that the two of them check in Sam's bedroom later.

She was cantering the colt along a barbed-wire fence when she heard a snort and the pounding of hooves. She glanced back in time to see the new bull

charge up behind her and the colt from the other side
of the fence. In the next instant, the bull hit the wire,
breaking through it with terrifying ease.

There was no time to spur the colt out of harm's
way. The moment the bull broke through the taut
wire, the impact yanked the top three strands free of
their staples. The broken wire recoiled, hissing
through the air in Rio's direction.

She had only a moment to throw her arm over her
face before the strands of wire whipped around her
and the colt. The colt squealed as the wire barbs
twisted into the hide of his chest and lashed his legs.
His sudden lunge into the air set the barbs deeper, and
his drop to earth tangled his front ankles.

The next few moments seemed to move in slow
motion as the colt continued to fight the wire. Rio
struggled to regain control of the young horse, but it
was a lost cause almost instantly. The wire slashed at
her, ripping her clothes and her skin. The animal's
irrational hop toward the intact section of fence next
to them caught him in more wire. He stumbled and
fell against the four-strand barbed-wire fence and sent
them both crashing to the ground.

She had no more than a second for the horse to
realize he was more tangled in wire than ever. Just
that quickly, he tried to thrash clear of the wire. It
took every bit of strength she had to pull the reins so
tight that at last the colt lay still.

Rio gasped for breath, dragging in quick little puffs
of air as the sharp barbs of the wire cut painfully
through her clothes and into her skin. Her left leg was
pinned under the colt, but the placement of the weath-

ered fence post he'd knocked down kept her leg from being crushed.

Wire curled over them both, lashing them to what was left of the fence and to each other. But the most dangerous piece of wire lay tight across Rio's right shoulder and angled snugly against the tender flesh of her throat. She tried to lift her left hand and wedge her fingers between the wire and her throat in hopes of pushing it away, but her arm was caught in the wire.

The only hand she had free was her right hand. The colt started struggling again, and it was all she could do to keep her grip firm on the reins as she tried to keep the frightened animal down. She couldn't risk letting go of the reins to get the wire away from her throat, but if she couldn't hold the horse...

Panic overwhelmed her as she held the reins tight and tried to carefully wiggle her left hand free. The sun pounded down hotly, and it surprised her a little to realize that she was already drenched with sweat. She murmured to the young horse, trying to calm him, though they were both shaking with the tremors that went through his big body.

The bull snorted nearby and she froze. She turned her head as far as she could and caught sight of the huge animal standing not a dozen feet away, his head down as he pawed the sod. The dust he stirred floated toward her like a low cloud.

"Oh, God, please—" She watched in horror as the bull continued to dig at the sod. He paused, then lifted his head and bellowed. The horse started at that, and

Rio felt his muscles bunch for another attempt at escape.

Tears of pain and frustration crowded into her eyes as she fought to hold the horse still. The wire barbs cut into her skin in what felt like dozens of places. Every time the horse moved, the barbs bit deeper, until she was hurting so much she almost couldn't lie still herself.

Just when she thought she couldn't hold the reins any tighter, the bull made a shuffling sound. Terrified, she looked over in time to see the huge beast take a step toward her. He took two lumbering strides then suddenly, amazingly, he turned and ambled off until he was out of the narrow view she had in that direction.

Relief stole her strength and she felt herself fairly melt against the ground. The restless move of the horse as he again tested the tautness of the wire made her go rigid again as she gripped the reins.

She laid there for what seemed like hours, murmuring to the colt, fighting to keep her grip on the reins while she tried to free her left hand and arm. The longer she lay there, the more pain made an impression.

Heat and thirst heightened her torment and dizzying fatigue compounded it. Every so often, she turned her head as far as the wire would allow, hoping she'd see another rider, but no one came.

She laid there for so long that she felt herself start to drift. The cloud that passed between her and the sun sent a small breath of coolness over her.

"Hey there, little girl—what is it you got yourself into?"

Sam's voice, strong and familiar, moved through her and her eyes sprang open to look for his face. The sun was bright behind his head and shoulders as he leaned over her. She couldn't see his face clearly, but the certainty that it was Sam comforted her so deeply that her fear immediately eased.

"Sam…"

"I'm here, baby," he assured her, "just lie still. That little sorrel will stay calm if you will."

How many times had she heard him say that to her when she'd worked a young horse? Just when she realized she was probably dreaming, he said, "Kane's comin'."

The slight move of her head caused her pain. "He doesn't know where I am," she rasped.

Sam's voice was confident. "He doesn't, but the Good Lord knows exactly where you are, honey."

"H-how are you here?" she got out, then swallowed convulsively at the painful dryness of her throat.

"As long as you remember, a part of me never really leaves. I'll always be there in your heart, in your memories—" The colt stirred and Sam told her, "You need to keep that rein tight, Rio, cause you can't come where I am for a good many years. You gotta lot of livin' ahead of you."

Rio's mouth was so dry that she merely moved her lips to say, "Please, Sam, come home." Her eyes were blurred but she could see him shake his head.

"I am home, sweet girl," he said gently. "I had

my time on the earth. Got myself a strong, healthy, young body again and a good baritone voice to sing in that big church choir up yonder. I'm only here now so you don't lose heart.''

Somehow it seemed important to let him know that she would hang on. She tried to tell him, but her mouth was too dry to get the words out.

"I know, Rio. I can tell," he said, as if he'd read her thoughts. "Ain't you named that colt yet?" he teased, then chuckled. "Might want to call him Barbie. Boz'll get a kick outta the name, 'specially after this."

Rio felt a smile pull at her lips, but she was drifting again and could hardly keep hold of the reins.

Sam's soft, "I'm leaving now, honey. Kane'll be here in a minute," made her stir, but she was so weak. She felt herself begin to sink and her fingers went slack. The coolness gusted over her face and, thinking Sam had come back, she forced her eyes open.

"Sam?"

Kane's voice was brisk. "Take it easy. I'm here."

Rio tried to focus on him. The sun was not nearly so bright now, and Kane leaned over her, his big body shading her face. "Sam was here," she got out, but her voice was barely a whisper.

Kane was growling at someone, cursing, and the colt began to shift on the ground. Rio tried to hold the reins, but they were no longer in her fingers.

"Get those damned cutters over here." Kane's voice sounded strange to her, but she couldn't focus sharply enough on his face to discern the reason. Kane moved, and she felt the tight wire that cut into her shoulder and across her throat go slack. It took her a moment to realize that the quiet snip she was hearing was the sound of a wire cutter.

The colt shifted again, and Kane swore. "If he won't lay quiet, shoot him."

The words penetrated her foggy thoughts and alarmed her. "No, please." She licked her dry lips and tried again. "Don't hurt him, Kane."

Kane grumbled something, then swore softly. Rio felt one wire after another snap loose. Once she could turn her head, she could see that there were three cowhands with Kane. He leaned close, then slid his hand beneath her shoulders to gently lift her.

Kane had never felt fear so strong that it made him gut sick, but seeing Rio on the ground in a bloody tangle of barbed wire with a frightened colt tangled up with her had done it. He hadn't been able to get to her quick enough to ease the terror he felt, the terror he still felt as they worked to free her from the wire.

She was already bleeding from a score of cuts, and he was suddenly terrified that she would bleed to death. When he slipped his hand beneath her shoulders to lift her in preparation for getting the colt off her leg, he felt the sticky wetness that had stiffened the back of her shirt and glued bits of grass and dirt to the fabric.

He glanced over at the cowhand who was getting ready to pull her leg free. Kane carefully lifted her until she was partially sitting up. The other two men had clipped the colt free of the wire and were positioning themselves to help the horse get up. At Kane's signal, the two men pushed the colt to his feet while he and the third ranch hand pulled Rio out of harm's way.

It was over in seconds. The colt was unsteady on his feet at first, then stood trembling as flies swarmed over his wounds. The man at his head coaxed him forward. He moved stiffly, favoring his left front leg.

Rio was limp in his arms, her eyes closed. One of the men brought a canteen and Kane trickled a bit of water onto her dry lips. The water roused her and she reached weakly for the canteen. Kane allowed her only two swallows before he took the water away.

"Sorry, baby," he murmured, "just a little at a time."

From there, it was a race to get Rio to a hospital. Kane carried her to the ranch pickup that Boz roared up in a few minutes later. By then, he'd sacrificed his shirt, tearing the sleeves out, then ripping it in a few strips to bind the wire cuts on her left arm and wrist. He used what was left as crude pads for the other deep cuts on her left side and back. By the time they got to the ranch headquarters, the helicopter from the nearest trauma center was touching down on the front lawn.

The paramedics took only a few minutes to check her vital signs and start an IV before the helicopter took off. Kane's last sight of Rio lying so still and frail and bloodied on the stretcher haunted him all the way to the hospital.

Rio lay uncomfortably in the private hospital room, her left arm and side sporting several inches of stitches. Her ribs, hip and leg were badly bruised, and her face and hands were sunburned. Her body temperature had been brought down, her blood pressure was in a good range, but the doctor had insisted on admitting her.

And she was weak. She'd managed to doze off a couple of times, but those brief naps had done nothing to strengthen her. Because she'd insisted on making her own trek to the bathroom a while ago, she knew precisely how weak she was and it had frightened her.

Kane was in the hospital somewhere, but so far he'd not come to her hospital room. He'd waited outside the trauma room for hours and she'd caught only an occasional glimpse of him as the doctor and nurses worked to lower her body temperature, then to stitch her many cuts. He'd come into the cubicle briefly a couple of times, but finally elected to sit in the hall out of the way.

On the other hand, visiting hours had just ended. Since it was nearly dark, Kane might have already started home. Because they were both early risers, she understood why he might want to spare himself the ninety-mile ride to the ranch at a late hour.

The idea that she was in the hospital alone sent her spirits downward. She was lying on her right side and tried to shift to find a more comfortable spot, but her battered body ached no matter how she tried to lay. In the end, she gave up and closed her eyes.

Booted steps outside her door roused her from the twilight of half-sleep, but when they stopped without coming into the room, she closed her eyes again, unable to help the disappointment she felt. This was a Texas hospital. Boots were common footwear. Kane's confident stride was as familiar to her as his face, but perhaps it was her imagination that had conjured the distinctive sound.

She thought again about Sam. She realized now, of course, that his visit that day had been a dream or maybe a delusion brought on by fear and heat and blood loss. But it had seemed so real. She'd actually heard his voice, or thought she had. Hadn't the way she'd strained to see him been real, either?

In the end, it didn't matter whether it had been a dream or a delusion. Sam hadn't really come back to her but, as he'd said, he would always be there in her heart, in her memories. *I am home, sweet girl,* he'd said. *I had my time on the earth. Got myself a strong, healthy, young body again and a good baritone voice to sing in that big church choir up yonder. I'm only here now so you don't lose heart...*

How comforting those words had been! Even though Sam hadn't really been able to say them himself, they were a balm to her heart and soothed the pain of losing him. His *Ain't you named that colt yet?* made her smile.

Kane hovered outside the door of Rio's room, reluctant to disturb her if she was asleep. It didn't surprise him to realize that the only place he wanted to be was in that room, watching over her. The protectiveness he'd secretly felt toward her for years was suddenly fierce. He'd never forget how helpless and hurt she'd looked lying in that wire. He'd never forget that in one blinding moment of emotional clarity, his turbulent feelings toward her had settled neatly into place.

And though his feelings toward her were more stormy and primitive than ever, he now knew exactly what he wanted from Rio Cory.

The wire was so tight, and it hurt so much. The colt was frantic. She tried to keep him calm, to hold the reins so tight he couldn't get up, but the bits of leather were slick, defying her effort to hang on to them. And the bull was charging toward them, faster and faster, closer and closer...

Rio cried out, the horror of the dream making her jerk as she flung up her arm to protect herself. It was several moments before she realized that she was lying in a hospital bed and that the big hands manacling her wrists were trying to help, not hurt.

A huge sob sent pain shooting everywhere. The familiar traces of Kane's after-shave made an impression before the low, gruff sound of his voice did. "Kane?"

"It's me, baby. You're safe."

"The bull was—" She belatedly cut herself off. The nightmare lingered, but reality was flooding back. Relief made her wilt against the pillow and Kane's grip on her wrists eased. The dim light coming from behind him made it difficult to see his face.

"What about the bull?" The terse question alerted Rio. She remembered then that she hadn't told anyone exactly how the accident happened. All they knew was that she and the horse she was riding had got caught in barbed wire.

Her concern for the colt made her ignore his question. "What about the colt? Is he all right?"

Now that her eyes were adjusting to the dimness, she saw the harsh lines of his face ease. "I talked to Boz this evening. The colt is about as cut up and battered as you, but he's okay." Kane's expression went grim again. "Though for two cents I feel like selling him, or better, sending him to the meat packer."

Rio was instantly alarmed. "What for?"

"For being enough of a bubble head to tangle you both in several feet of barbed wire. What'd he do, take off in a bucking fit and try to go through the fence?"

Kane's assessment of the circumstances of the accident stunned her, but the consequences he seemed so anxious to carry out upset her.

"No—you can't do that, Kane. He's a good little horse," she told him quickly.

"And you're too softhearted and sentimental," he growled.

Rio shook her head, then winced at the pain. "It wasn't his fault."

Kane's expression was stony. "Then whose fault was it?"

"It was the new bull." The moment she said the words and saw the impact they had on Kane, she wished she'd found a much less blunt way to tell him. Kane not only placed a high value on the animal, he'd spent a fortune for him. The dangerous gleam in his eyes suggested that he was furious suddenly. The fear that Kane was angry with her—again—made her heart sink. Rio pressed her lips together, reluctant to tell him more.

"So what happened?" Kane was brisk with her, all business, and his steely tone made her dread his reaction more than she already did.

"We were riding along the fence. I didn't know the bull was in the next pasture until I heard him coming up behind us from the other side of the fence." Rio told him the rest, quailing inwardly at the dark anger on Kane's face. And because she was anxious to be certain the colt wouldn't somehow be blamed, she added, "The colt probably handled it as well as a more seasoned horse, given his inexperience. He was frightened and he was in pain. I don't know how much time passed, but he stayed on the ground a long time. I either passed out or fell asleep at least once. He could have taken advantage of that."

She went silent. There was no need to say more. Besides, she'd never seen the kind of anger—no, rage—she was seeing in Kane's eyes now. He couldn't be that angry with the colt, so it had to be her he was furious with. He was probably thinking she could have been more alert to the bull's approach, or that she should have been able to keep the colt from panicking and falling into the fence.

Years of not measuring up, of loving Kane and knowing he was forever beyond her reach, brought a suspicious fullness to her eyes. She'd failed again in his sight, and she was so exhausted and uncomfortable and heartsore over losing Sam that this new failure was more than she could bear.

She put up her right hand and covered her eyes,

mortified that she was on the verge of bursting into tears. Her hoarse, "I'm really tired, could you leave now?" ended on a sob that sent sharp pain through her bruised ribs.

Kane plucked her hand from her face the very instant the tears began to seep over her lashes. She glanced up into his harsh face before her eyes shied from the strange dismay in his.

"And I'm sorry. Again," she blurted, then clenched her teeth together to get control of herself. She tried to pull her hand from his, but his firm grip made it impossible. Frustration made the tears come faster. "D-damn it—will you let me go and leave me alone?"

Kane released her hand and Rio quickly used it to brush impatiently at the hot tears cascading down her cheeks. The bed jerked a bit, and she realized that Kane had lowered the side rail. She was about to edge away when he leaned over her and braced his hands on either side of her head to come close, his lips a hand span from hers.

Rio pushed her hand against his chest to force him away, but he was immovable. She read his intent in the hot gleam of his eyes before his lips closed the distance and toyed softly with hers.

"Don't do this, Kane, please," she got out as she tried to turn her face from his. His hand on her cheek kept her from evading him while his lips continued to flirt with hers. She groaned, then slipped her fingers up to press over his mouth to keep it from touching hers.

"I can't take this, Kane," she whispered brokenly.

"I can't make my heart hard like you can, I can't make myself stop—" She cut herself off before she made another foolish confession of love.

But she dissolved into tears anyway, unable to suppress the weak, wounded sobs that sent stabbing pains into her bruised side for those first few moments. Kane sat on the bed and gathered her carefully into his arms. She was too weak physically and emotionally to fight him any longer, and so she clung to his shirtfront and cried.

It was heaven and hell to be held by him, just as it had always been heaven and hell to be anywhere near him. She was too exhausted to grapple with the insanity, too broken to try to analyze it. Kane knew her most important secrets anyway, so he had surely detected the pleasure/pain of her feelings for him.

By the time the crying jag had spent itself, she was limp in his arms and so weak she could hardly move. Kane laid her back on the pillow, then grabbed a tissue from the side table and blotted her sunburned cheeks.

Rio didn't open her eyes. She lay still for a few moments after he finished, then felt him lean toward her. His minty breath gusted softly over her face before his lips again settled on hers.

The firm caress of his mouth as it moved masterfully over hers sent a reviving heat through her. Rio's eyes came open, then fell shut as his mouth moved demandingly on hers. Her fingers found the hand he'd braced beside her head. She slid her palm beneath his and felt their fingers lace together.

The pressure of his lips eased and he pulled back

slightly to rasp, "I'm going to have you, Rio. Soon. Today changed things between us, and I'm done fighting the urge." He brought a hand up and trailed a finger along her jaw. He let the finger drop to the front of her gown and traced a line to her breast. His eyes were like blue flames. "You get well, Rio Cory. You get strong." His lips descended swiftly to hers and his kiss left her breathless. He withdrew slowly. Rio's eyes opened and clung to the fiery intensity of his. He pulled his fingers from hers and raised the bed rail.

"Sleep tight, baby. I'll be back before breakfast." And then he was gone.

CHAPTER NINE

RAMONA had been frantic to find the book. She'd secretly read about it in Sam's letter to Rio, so she knew what was supposed to be in it. Now that she'd finally found it, she was beside herself with excitement. Quietly, she lifted it from its resting place in the bottom drawer of Sam's dresser.

She'd searched all over for the key to the damned drawer—the last place in the house where the book could possibly be. She must have gone through every pocket, shelf and potential hiding place before she'd found it. It had been hanging by a string among Sam's collection of ties. She never would have noticed it had she not got frustrated with the search and slapped spitefully at the ties to muss them.

The moment she'd discovered the key was the moment that her daring plan was assured of success. Ramona felt good about this, clever, superior. In the past few days she'd become quite good at going through the private papers of others to find what she wanted. Not even the witch sisters, Ardis and Estelle, had been able to catch her at it.

Ramona set the book carefully on the bed. It was stuffed so full of dead flowers and papers and photos that it would never lay flat, and that annoyed her. How could you find one specific thing among such a collection of garbage? Only someone pathetic enough and sentimental enough to examine each page would ever find anything specific.

Fortunately, Rio Cory was pathetic enough and sentimental enough. And because she was, she was certain to find out the ugly truth in the book all by herself. Ramona only had to make sure that the truth was there before Rio got the book.

Kane came back before breakfast that next morning as he'd promised, but the doctor didn't come to examine her until midmorning. By then, the floral delivery man had come by her room and left her a dozen red roses in an expensive Lalique crystal vase. Rio had assumed they were from Kane until she read the card.

Kane's face had been rock-hard when she'd glanced up from reading it. His gruff, "Who's the romantic?" made her hesitate to tell him.

She said nothing, but passed him the card. Kane took it, and to her chagrin, read it aloud. "'Glad you're all right. Will make it up to you. Ty.'" He virtually sneered the name before he glared over at her. "Sounds like I need to make sure everyone knows you've been cut out of the herd."

Rio's gaze fled his. She loved Kane with all her heart, but what he'd proposed the night before shamed her. The thrill of his declaration to "have" her died the moment she realized that no declaration of love or proposal of marriage had followed it. He'd said he was tired of fighting the urge. Urges were more lust than love.

She deliberately ignored his statement and instead

gazed at the roses. "How did he know I was in the hospital?"

"I told him when I offered him the bull back."

Rio glanced over at him, surprised. "What?"

"I offered him the bull. On the hoof for a price, or over a barbecue pit for Labor Day."

Rio was shaking her head before he finished. "That bull is too valuable. You'll never get your investment back if you sell him at a loss—and it will be a loss. It will also be a waste to slaughter him."

Kane's gruff "Money doesn't matter, he could have killed you," gave her heart a pang. She knew Kane was upset that she'd been hurt, but not because he was madly in love with her. Suddenly bitter, she gave him a cynical look, angry at herself for loving him so foolishly and angry at him for not being able to love her.

"You don't have to grandstand," she told him quietly. "You don't need to worry about my health, either. I've already seen a lawyer and made a will. If I should die, my half of Langtry will go directly to you. If I become disabled somehow, and I'm not able to fully participate as your co-owner, I've signed papers that give you the authority to act for me. Sam's will won't have been violated, you won't have an animal rights group on your back, and you can live happily ever after."

Kane's face had gone dark. He was furious. "What the hell's the matter with you?" he growled.

Rio expelled a weary breath, but her gaze didn't waver from his. "Maybe I'm wising up." She'd already considered what she wanted to say. Now was the time to say it. "So you'll need to keep fighting that 'urge' you mentioned last night. Exciting as it might be, I won't have an affair with you. You already have my love, and you might always have that, but I won't give you what's left of my self-respect."

The sadness she felt made her look away from the blue flare of outrage in his eyes. Fortunately, the doctor strode into the room. A nurse shooed Kane to the hall, and the doctor made his examination.

The nurse helped her dress in the clean clothes Kane had brought, gave her two bottles of medications plus prescriptions for more should she need them. She brushed and braided Rio's hair, then helped her into the wheelchair. Rio held the crystal vase of roses on her lap as the nurse wheeled her out.

By the time Kane got her settled in the car, she was worn out. Kane was still furious with her, the air between them was turbulent with it. He only spoke to her when necessary all the way to Langtry.

When they arrived, Rio tried to get out of the car by herself, but she was so stiff and sore she'd barely got the door open before Kane came around to her side of the car. Despite her protest, he carefully slid one hand behind her back and one under her knees before he lifted her out.

Rio couldn't help but notice that his profile was rigid with bad temper. Neither of them spoke as he carried her up the walk, then in the front door that Estelle held open for them. He ignored Ramona and Tracy, who'd come out of the living room as he stalked past, his no-nonsense glare keeping them all silent.

Tension and dread distracted Rio from the discomfort of being moved around as Kane carried her up the stairs. A confrontation was coming, that was certain. More heartache would follow, that was also certain.

When they reached her room, Kane got the door open, then carried her in. He paused to kick the door shut before he walked over to her bed. He sat her gently on the bedspread, then towered over her. Impatiently, he reached up to yank his hat off and toss it toward a chair.

"So you don't want an affair, huh?"

Rio looked up at him. Kane Langtry was a ruggedly handsome, virile man. The longing to have him make love to her was suddenly so sharp that she almost reached for him then. Her body hungered for whatever he could give her for as long as he wanted to give it, but sadly, she knew her heart could never withstand physical intimacy without love. She'd never survive the pain when he tired of her and pushed her out of his life. Her eyes stung. "I love you, Kane, but enough is enough."

He hunkered down in front of her and she had to make herself meet his solemn gaze. He touched her hand and she eased it away.

"I reckon I deserve for you to think that I'm a complete S.O.B.," he growled. "I've acted like one long enough to qualify." He lifted his hand and slid two fingers into his shirt pocket. When he brought them out, something bright sparkled between his fingertips. "But I'm in love with you, Rio Cory. I don't want an affair with you, either. I want you to be my wife.''

It took a moment for her to realize that Kane had proposed marriage. He rolled the band of the ring between his thumb and finger so that the huge diamond winked boldly at her, drawing her attention. The ring was magnificent. What it represented made her breathless, but heartache brought her back to earth and she forced herself to look at him.

''But you hate wanting me,'' she whispered sadly. ''You said yourself that I'm the last woman you want.''

''I've had too much control over my life to appreciate losing my head over a woman. None of the others ever made me feel anything I couldn't walk away from, so I hated it when I realized you had some special power over me.''

Rio glanced away, not certain she could believe what she was hearing. Perhaps the accident had somehow pushed her over the edge and she was imagining this as she'd imagined Sam coming to her. Kane placed a finger under her chin and silently coaxed her to look at him. It took her a moment to find the courage.

''You were nineteen when I started comparing other women to you,'' he said, his voice husky and low. ''But none of them had eyes like sapphires or hair so long and thick that a man aches to wrap his hands in it. None of the others was as beautiful or as loyal and smart as you, none of them made my heart race and made me dream wild dreams.''

Rio was stunned. Oh, God, what he was saying was a miracle, but she was terrified of being disappointed.

Kane ran the back of his knuckle gently along her jaw as his look grew somber. "I almost lost you yesterday, baby. I found out then that there are scarier things than what I feel for you."

Joy burst in her heart but Rio's gaze fell from his as she automatically tried to conceal it from him. Everything he was saying to her was wonderful, but they'd lived at odds for too long for her not to be wary.

Kane's softly spoken, "Rio?" made her look at him again. "If it's not too late for me—for us—then marry me, honey. You'll never regret it."

She looked deep into the dark blue of his eyes, searching for love, searching for the truth. All she could see was the utter sincerity of the man she'd loved for nearly half her life, the man whose heart was too hard won to doubt. She lifted her hand and placed it on his hard jaw, terrified, nonetheless.

"We've both been through a lot lately, what with Sam..." She had to pause a moment because it was still hard to verbally acknowledge his death. "And then the accident shook us both up." She watched Kane's expression grow hard as she went on, "I know you Texas men are loathe to consider it, but maybe our emotions aren't what we think they a—"

The sudden advance of Kane's mouth cut her off. His lips fastened on hers with a fervency that stole her breath. When he finally withdrew, she couldn't think straight.

"You've loved me for a long time and I've loved

you,'' he growled. ''It didn't start yesterday or last week or last month. I doubt very much that either one of us will ever wake up one day and decide that what we feel now was some kind of emotional overreaction or a byproduct of grief for my father.''

Kane lifted his hand and held the ring between them. One side of his handsome mouth kicked up in a half grin. ''If it's the ring you don't like, you can pick out something else. I can have the jeweler bring a selection to Langtry before supper.''

Rio released a short, surprised breath and shook her head. ''It's beautiful, Kane,'' she whispered.

''Then will you marry me, or do you need to think about it?''

She felt herself melt as she stared into the intensity in his eyes. She recognized the look, the unyielding resolve of a strong, powerful man who decides what he wants and goes after it. It reassured her to see that in Kane and to know that she was the focus of that resolve.

Her quiet, ''I'll marry you,'' was barely audible.

Kane's intense expression relaxed and he reached for her hand. Rio felt a bit dazed as she watched him gently slide the ring on her finger. He lifted her hand and placed a tender kiss on the back of it.

He looked into her eyes then, his gaze hot and sensual. He kissed her hand again, then turned it over and kissed her palm, all the while watching her face to gauge her reaction. Rio leaned toward him and he met her lips with a kiss so tender and profound that it flooded her heart with joy.

*　　*　　*

The world had shifted on its axis. It was the same sun, the same moon and stars, the same year and month, the same house and ranch, the same people involved who had always been involved—and yet everything had changed. Kane had changed and Rio realized she was changing because he had. The world was new suddenly, and she felt like a child at Christmas.

Kane Langtry loved her at last and though he was not publicly demonstrative, everyone saw instantly the change in their relationship.

Ramona noticed right away and her reaction to the news of their engagement surprised Rio almost as much as Kane's proposal had. The older woman gave every impression of being delighted with the match, even going so far as to volunteer to help with the wedding or to recommend a wedding planner.

Tracy seemed as aloof as ever, though she coolly offered her best wishes and seconded her mother's offer of assistance. Ardis and Estelle reacted reservedly to the news, as they always did, but it pleased Rio when they started making plans for a thorough deep cleaning of the house for the wedding reception and began to pester Kane about making a few decorating changes.

The days following the riding accident passed swiftly for Rio. Though she was still quite sore from the stitches and bruises, she wasn't one to lie around and wait for herself to heal. She couldn't ride yet or do outside ranch work, but paperwork suited her. She did her best to work the soreness from her abused body by walking and doing simple exercises. The removal of the stitches made increased activity a bit easier, and by the end of the second week, she was riding for short periods of time.

Kane was wonderful to her. He took her along on two day-long business trips, one to Austin, the other to Dallas. Both days, he finished business by noon, then took her to lunch and shopping. While Kane had been in his morning meetings, she'd checked on wedding consultants in both cities, selected one, then immediately panicked at the number of things that needed to be done.

"Hell, I've heard for years about the pomp and bother of big-ticket weddings," Kane told her as they flew home from Dallas. "But I figure to be married only one time, and since I aim for you to marry only one time, I'd like our big-ticket wedding to be something along the lines of spectacular."

That said, he smiled over at her doubtful expression, then reached over and caught her hand. "Come on, baby. I'm proud to marry you and I want everyone in Texas to know it. That wedding consultant you hired can take care of the headaches. All you'll have to do is put on the dress, walk down the aisle, then promise to love and obey."

That startled a laugh from Rio. "I thought it was the groom who promised that," she told him.

Kane shook his head adamantly. "No you don't— the traditional vows suit me just fine," he declared, then looked over at her, a gleam of laughter in his eyes. He tugged on her hand and brought it to his lips to kiss the back of her fingers before he returned his full attention to flying.

Rio settled deeper in her seat, marveling at the easy companionship between them, grateful beyond words that they were no longer at odds with each other. She still missed Sam terribly, but her new closeness to Kane eased the hurt.

Sam had told her in the letter that he'd somehow know when they settled their differences. She wasn't certain he'd had in mind a marriage between them when he'd written the letter, but plans to marry certainly signified a level of harmony and cooperation they'd never had while he'd been alive. The reminder gave her a pang. How much better it would have been for them to come to this point while Sam had been around to enjoy it. On the other hand, it had happened at last. Rio hoped Sam really did know about it somehow.

As had become their habit, Kane slipped into her room later that night just before their early bedtime. He was there waiting when she emerged from her shower and the bathroom.

He was lying on her bed with his shoulders braced against the headboard, his hands resting on his lean middle and his legs crossed at the ankles. His blue gaze was smoky with desire as he watched her walk out of the bathroom and cross to the side of the bed. His lips twisted faintly. "That bathrobe ought to wear out one of these days, baby. If it doesn't in time for the wedding, I promise to burn it."

Rio couldn't help the shy, pleased smile on her face. Kane had a difficult time reining in his libido, but he did. He understood her reluctance to preview their wedding night. But although he complied with her wishes, he either made up outrageous stories about how debilitating abstinence was for Texas males, or he came up with new destruction scenarios for her robe.

Rio gave him a look of mock reproof, then pointed at his feet. "Boots off the bed, cowboy."

A slow smile spread across his handsome mouth. "Make me, darlin'." The sultry look he gave her was an enticement to come closer.

When she hesitated, his hand shot out and caught the hem of the terry-cloth robe. She reached down to catch his hand as he pulled on the robe to draw her closer. Suddenly he seized her wrist. Just that quickly he pulled her down on top of him then rolled over, neatly pinning her beneath him.

She answered his gruff, "Am I hurting you?" with a slight shake of her head.

His mouth opened voraciously over hers, urging hers to open and respond before he deepened the kiss and his tongue did a strong imitation of what they both ached for. Rio was breathless before he eased his lips from hers and slid down her body to nibble at her neck. The expertise of his hand beneath her robe made her tremble.

"Oh, please, Kane—it's wonderful," she panted. Then, frustrated with herself, rasped a pained, "S-stop."

Kane complied, but slowly. She could feel the tension and hardness of his body and realized dazedly that this time, they'd almost instantly reached the point of no return. It didn't take much anymore for a kiss or a touch to send them soaring, and she began to have real worries about being able to wait until their wedding night. She had just as many worries about whether she might perish from frustrated desire before they could get to the altar.

Kane growled against her neck and slid his hand from beneath her robe. "Damn, baby, one of us needs to move that wedding date, or we won't have a snowball's chance of making it."

"T-the soonest is four weeks from Saturday," she stammered, absolutely horrified that four weeks wasn't much time to pull off the huge wedding Kane seemed to want.

Kane's groan was so eloquent that it made her giggle. He lifted his head and looked down at her. "That sounds nice. And that smile. Just wraps around my heart, darlin', and makes me feel fine." He lowered his head and feathered a few gentle kisses over her lips. "I love you."

Rio felt her heart burst. Kane told her regularly now that he loved her, and each time he said it was more thrilling than the last. Her soft, "I love you," was almost painful because the words were so inadequate to express what she felt for him. She reached up with both hands and slid her fingers into his thick, dark hair. She lifted her head from the pillow and pressed her lips against his, starved for the taste of him.

Kane kissed her back and Rio melted beneath him until, reluctantly, he pulled away. "This would probably be a good time to give you what I found. Otherwise…"

He rubbed his jaw on her cheek, then eased off her and rolled to his back. He rested his forearm over his eyes and gave a deep sigh. They both lay quietly, and though they were no longer touching, Rio could feel her body straining toward the male heat of his.

Kane reached for her hand and gave it a squeeze before he sat up and got off the bed. Rio rolled to her side and tried to hold her robe together as she followed. She stood by the bed as Kane walked to her dresser. When she glanced past him and saw the huge book, she sprinted after him.

"Is this the book Sam left for me?" The question was an outburst of surprise and delight because it was plain that it was. Though the title *Plant and Animal Species of the World* was the one Sam had indicated, it was also obvious that the book was so crammed with pressed flowers that its cover would never lie flat.

"Sorry it took so long. I didn't find a key until this evening. I was about to pry the lock on the drawer I thought it might be in, when I remembered a collection of old cabinet keys Estelle keeps in a pantry drawer. One of them worked in the lock."

Rio touched the book then slipped her fingers under the edge of the front cover and carefully opened it. The first thing she saw was a photograph of her mother and five other women at a Langtry barbecue. The other women were each holding up a dessert they'd made. Her mother was holding up a tall chocolate layer cake.

It startled Rio to see the picture. She'd never realized how much she looked like her mother. She'd seen other pictures, so she'd known there was a strong resemblance, but it was even more evident in this photo.

"You and your mama could be taken for twins. She was a beautiful, tenderhearted woman," Kane said quietly as he looked on. "He was in love with her, you know."

Rio looked over at Kane. "I didn't know, exactly. He spoke fondly of her." She paused and glanced down to turn a page. "But until I realized he and my mother were going to be buried next to each other..." She shook her head. "I can't think of a single time that I ever saw them touch or talk about anything other than the weather or her garden or her health, and yet, now I feel the strangest..." She paused and turned another page.

She carefully leafed through the first few pages. The flowers were dry and frail. She suddenly had a mental picture of Sam's big, calloused hands tenderly laying each stem and bloom between the pages. For all his tough, rugged looks, and hard-edged masculinity, Sam Langtry had had a core of gentleness and compassion that you didn't suspect when you looked at him.

Her eyes filled with tears and she blinked them back to turn another page. A small square of blue plaid cotton had been smoothed between these pages. From the look of it, probably taken off the wire barb that had torn it from a dress. Rio touched the fabric. Shapes cut from the same fabric had been pieced into the quilt top in her mother's sewing box.

Kane's voice was low, almost hushed. "How sentimental does a man have to be about a woman to press flowers she's grown in a book and keep them all these years?"

It wasn't really a question he expected an answer to and Rio didn't answer it. "Sam never said anything to me," she said quietly.

"He didn't say anything to me, either. I knew he thought she was a fine woman and too good for Ned, but I never would have known he was in love with her if I hadn't overheard them talking."

Rio turned her head to look at him. "When was this? What did they say?" She was suddenly hungry to know. She couldn't imagine a more perfect childhood than if Sam and her mother had married. Because her father had been so abusive, the reminder that her mother would have had to divorce him to marry Sam didn't bother her.

"You must have been about seven, because I was seventeen. I knew your mother was going to take you down to one of the hay barns to see a new litter of kittens. My father must have joined her there, because I was walking up from the creek and heard them."

Rio carefully closed the book and gave Kane her complete attention. "What did they say?"

Kane glanced away a moment as he remembered. "Lenore's voice was shaky, which got my attention, since she was always so cheerful, even when she didn't have much to be cheerful about. She was saying, 'We're both people who honor the Good Book too much to let our emotions lead us, Sam. I know Ned's not much as a husband or provider, but I made vows with him before God.'" Kane's gaze came back to hers. "That's when I heard my father say that he'd never put her in a position to choose. He told her he'd love her till his dying day, but unless she became free, he'd keep his feelings to himself.''

Rio's lips parted in shock at the enormity of what Kane was telling her. She left the book on the dresser, then walked, stunned, toward the bed and sat down on the edge as she tried to recover.

''Then they were in love with each other,'' she whispered as she looked over at Kane.

''For all the good it did either of them,'' he said darkly. ''I think it about killed him when she got sick and died. He got the very best doctors for her, but there was no hope.'' Kane went silent for a long time. Rio glanced away and didn't speak, either.

She was suddenly awash with memories of her father's drunkenness and his terrible temper. She still had dim memories of him backhanding her mother or shoving her around. Most times, it seemed he barely noticed there was even a child in the house, much less that the child was his. ''Why didn't she do something? Why didn't she divorce my father?''

''Too much honor, I reckon,'' he said solemnly. ''She'd made a vow she felt bound to keep. My father apparently couldn't bring himself to steal another man's wife, no matter how bad a husband she had.''

Kane's lips quirked humorlessly. ''Old-fashioned morality at its most noble and most painful. You don't often hear about honor like that these days. I admire their restraint.''

''And that's why they're buried so close now,'' she guessed.

Kane nodded. ''Reckon so.''

Rio's eyes stung as she looked over at the book.

"Thanks for finding it for me. If you'd like, you can look through it yourself." She was so overcome with emotion that she had to push the words out.

"I think I'd like to save it for another day, when it's not so late in the evening and Dad's passing isn't quite so fresh." He paused, then walked over to the bed and crouched down before her to take her hand. "And I'd rather you took it in small doses yourself. I don't think he left it for you to make you sad."

Rio reached up and put her hand on Kane's hard jaw, touched by his concern. "I know," she whispered. "I probably can't get through all of it in one sitting anyway. It looks like there're other things besides flowers in it. On top of which," she said, then took a bracing breath, "I'm still a little in shock about finding out that they were in love with each other."

"Are you gonna be all right?" he asked gently, and she nodded. He smiled at her. "All right then, baby, give me a kiss to last till morning."

Rio smiled then and leaned forward to touch his lips with hers.

CHAPTER TEN

Two days later, Kane went to Dallas on business. Since he planned to be there for the next few days, Rio stayed behind to meet with the wedding planner and draw up a guest list.

Their foreman took over for them both while Rio met with the planner and her assistant. To her relief, one of the few tasks left for her to do in preparation for the wedding was to select her gown and those of her bridesmaids. Her two closest friends, whom she'd met at college, had been thrilled to hear she was marrying Kane and that she wanted them to be her bridesmaids.

She made a quick trip to Austin to shop for the dresses, then decided not to choose until she'd seen what else was available in Dallas.

It was while she was packing an overnight bag for a trip to Dallas to shop for a dress and to drop in briefly at Kane's office there, that she glanced over at the book Sam had left for her. Kane had been right about going through the book slowly. She'd already found a couple of notes to Sam from her mother. One was in a sympathy card Lenore had sent when Sam's cousin had died, the second was about the doctor's prognosis of her illness. Both had made her more emotional, and she'd found that giving herself a

156

chance to absorb each new thing was preferable to one long, intense session.

Because she was planning to be gone until late the next day, she finished packing and carefully leafed through the next few pages of pressed flowers, until she came to a page with a single sheet of paper wedged in the seam.

She knew at first glance that it was a birth certificate. The raised stamp of the notary public authenticated the document. She saw her given name, Rhea René Cory, her birth date and the Texas city and county she'd been born in, before her eyes skimmed over the names of her parents.

The name *Samuel Kendall Langtry* jumped out at her. At first, her mind refused the words. A hot, painful pressure began in her chest and shot upward to the top of her head. Her hands started to shake. *Samuel Kendall Langtry.*

No matter how many times she forced her eyes to read the name, it didn't change. Instead of Ned Cory's name in the space where her father's name should be, Sam Langtry's name was neatly typed.

Panicked, she snatched up the document and examined it closely, as if by doing so Sam's name would suddenly become Ned Cory's instead. The name didn't change and the horror she felt made her nauseous.

It took several minutes for her brain to start working again. She remembered the boxes of her mother's things still sitting in her closet. All Lenore's legal papers were there, and Rio felt a glimmer of hope. Of course—her real birth certificate had to be in the small metal box. She'd needed it when she'd got her driver's license and again for college, hadn't she?

She rushed to the closet, yanked the door open and switched on the light. The huge walk-in was more room than closet. It easily held the personal things she hadn't had time to return to the attic, as well as the few boxes of her mother's things.

In moments, she'd found the metal box. She fumbled with the key that had been taped to it, then opened the lid. Her fear and frustration mounted as she flipped through the small selection of papers until she found a folded document at the very bottom of the box.

Rio set the box aside and quickly unfolded the paper. The name Ned Cory was printed neatly in the space where it should have been, and her relief was so profound that she sagged against the wall.

But the movement made the light and shadow cast by the overhead fixture shift over the printed lines. The tiny marks around her father's name caught her attention. She straightened, her heart thumping wildly as a new wave of panic shot through her.

She rushed back into her room for the lamp on the bedside table. She switched on the lamp, then lifted off the lampshade to hold the birth certificate up to the bulb. The series of white marks beneath the dark print were plainly visible. What must have been the white print from correction tape spelled out enough letters on either side of Ned Cory's name for her to read. *Samuel Kendall Langtry.*

Rio lowered the paper. She walked shakily to the dresser and picked up the other birth certificate to take to the lamp for comparison. Both of the notarized documents were identical. Except for the correction tape letters on the one with Ned Cory's name typed over them, the original name in the father space on both documents was Samuel Kendall Langtry.

Rio set the documents down, her head spinning, her body quaking. She barely made it into her bathroom before she became violently ill.

Rio moved through the rest of the morning in a fog, her heart so turbulent with emotion that she was perpetually nauseous. The pain was unbelievable. The horror of realizing she was madly in love with her own half-brother devastated her.

The bitter sense of betrayal added more torment. She'd loved Sam as the father she'd never had, loved and trusted and devoted herself to him. But he'd known all along that he was her real father, or he couldn't have placed a copy of her birth certificate in the book he'd left for her to find. Why had he done that? Why had he allowed her to find out this way?

The letter he'd left for her said, *You've been everything a man could want in a daughter... Remember that I love you, my precious daughter...* The words had been a beautiful compliment when she'd read them. Now they seemed to be a confession of sorts. Perhaps he'd written them to prepare her for what he'd planned for her to find later.

Though she'd never told Sam directly, she'd been certain he'd somehow known that she was in love with Kane. Why hadn't he warned her away from her own brother? The shock of it made her head swim, and yet it was unbelievable that Sam could do such a thing.

She and Kane had marveled at Sam's restraint, she remembered bitterly. The way he and her mother had placed honor and morality above their own desires had been admirable. But the sad truth was that their parents' sense of honor and morality had evidently come late in their relationship. *Too late.*

Rio couldn't imagine telling Kane what she'd discovered. She couldn't bear to put the hellish burden of horror and guilt on Kane that was causing her such agony.

Oh, God, if there was a way to stop the engagement, yet spare him the truth, she had to find it! Anything had to be better for Kane than knowing he'd been planning to marry his own half-sister.

None of the others ever made me feel anything I couldn't walk away from...you had some special power over me, he'd said. Remembering the words increased her agony. He shouldn't love her, he couldn't love her. She'd loved him almost half her life and she was terrified she'd never be able to stop loving him.

Somehow she had to spare him that, she thought wildly. It would be better for Kane, and perhaps some small comfort to her, if he suddenly hated her.

Rio ended up packing a second bag. On her way downstairs with her luggage, she took a stealthy detour to Kane's room and slipped inside. She propped the note she'd written in the middle of the marble tray on his dresser, then set the beautiful engagement ring he'd given her next to it.

Because everyone in the house knew she was driving to Dallas today, she didn't bother to tell anyone goodbye. She carried her bags directly to the big garage, stowed them in the trunk, then got her car out. In seconds she was speeding down the ranch road, heartbroken to have to leave Langtry and everything she'd ever loved.

Kane,
I'm sorry to tell you this way, but I'm afraid I can't go through with our engagement or the wedding. I feel like the spoiled brat who cries for a toy until she gets it, then suddenly loses interest because the toy isn't as wonderful as she thought, or she finds something newer and shinier.

I've left the phone number of my new attorney below in case you need to get in contact with me. Don't worry about my half of the ranch going to the animal rights people. I'm not refusing the inheritance. We can just say that I've taken Sam's death hard and that I need to get away from the ranch for a while.

I think I might go to Colorado. I've hardly been off Langtry my whole life, except for college, and I'd like to see the mountains. Or maybe I'll go to Paris, since I took a year of French. I'll call in a few weeks.

Rio

Kane was brutally tired from his trip and the taxing flight he'd had coming home. One of the engines on the small plane hadn't been running right and air turbulence had been strong. Rio's note hit him like a two-by-four across the chest. He read it again, then growled long and low.

If he hadn't been so tired, he'd have seen past the toy analogy. He'd have realized that everything was even more desperately wrong than it appeared. Particularly when Rio, who craved the massive spaces and distances of Langtry, suddenly wanted to go to Paris. He wouldn't remember for days that she'd never taken a French course in her life.

Rio was numb and she welcomed the lack of feeling.

But if her heart was numb, her mind was roiling with confusion.

Had she been born before or after Ned and Lenore married? Had Ned known all along that she wasn't his child? Why had her mother married Ned instead of Sam?

She knew so little of her parents' backgrounds and families due to their early deaths and lack of information that she had no idea what the answers were.

She couldn't stop thinking about Kane. How was he? Had he found her note? Was he angry? Did he hate her now?

Rio ruthlessly stopped the questions before she could feel the pain they caused her. It had been three weeks since she'd fled Langtry. Though she checked in regularly with her lawyer, Kane had only placed one call to him. As instructed, the attorney had declined to answer Kane's demand to know where she was.

Even if the lawyer had told precisely where she

was, she would have been gone from there by the next morning. She'd rarely spent more than one night anywhere since she'd left the ranch. She'd been driven before by grief and restlessness when she'd roamed Langtry back home. The difference now was that a much greater pain drove her.

Instead of running toward the soothing vistas of the land, she'd fled to the much more complicated vistas of the big city. If there was any way to stop loving Kane, she had to find it.

Rio was sitting in a small, comfortable restaurant in San Antonio one afternoon. Her appetite was even worse in the heat, so she'd only ordered a large iced tea. She was moodily stirring the ice cubes with a straw, her spirits as downcast as ever, when someone stopped by her table.

"Is that you, Miz Rio?"

Ty Cameron's voice was a low, smooth drawl, but it startled Rio to hear her name. She glanced up and forced herself to smile at the handsome rancher.

"May I join you, or are you waiting for someone?" he asked her next.

Rio shook her head and made a tense gesture toward the chair across from her. "Please sit down, Mr. Cameron. I'd be pleased for you to join me."

She felt heat climb her cheeks as Ty sat down and his blue eyes met hers full-on. She should have known better than to come to San Antonio, but she'd felt as if she'd been nearly every place else in Texas these past weeks. Because Ty Cameron was also a businessman who traveled widely, their paths might just as easily have crossed in Dallas or Houston as in San Antonio. On the other hand, being seen by him in San Antonio might project a different message than if she'd met him in another city.

"Did you decide to come down and see what we do for fun in my little part of the country?"

Rio couldn't help noticing how good-looking Ty was. Or that his gaze was intense with male interest.

"I'm taking a sort of vacation," she said awkwardly. "I thought it might be nice to see some of the state."

Ty's gaze gleamed with curiosity the smallest moment before he gave her an easy smile. "I'd be proud to show you around."

Rio gave a tiny shake of her head and a rueful twist of lips. "Thanks, but my feet are already two sizes larger than they were this morning," she told him, then took a nervous sip of her iced tea.

His smile widened as he leaned back in his chair. "What you need is a quiet, comfortable place to put your feet up so you're in a better position to get spoiled. Since hotels and motels tend to lose their novelty quick, I'd like to ask you to come out to the ranch. You can have your pick of guest rooms, and I got a gal who runs my house who's not only the best cook in Texas, but the most dedicated chaperone in the whole southwest."

Rio couldn't help but get the message. Ty was perceptive enough to realize that she'd never consider staying at his ranch unless there were other people around. The mention of a dedicated chaperone was meant to put her at ease and show his respect for her. It also hinted that he might have romantic intentions.

The automatic refusal she wanted to give him suddenly stuck in her throat. She'd been traveling for weeks, lonely and suffering the worst emotional pain of her life. Ty Cameron was a gentleman. She was mildly attracted to him, and he apparently was mildly attracted to her.

It was either common sense or desperation that reminded her that she had little hope of letting go of her love for Kane or loving anyone else, unless she made an attempt to get to know someone new.

She toyed with her straw as she made herself give him a small smile. "Thank you, Mr. Cameron. I think I'd enjoy visiting your ranch."

Cameron Ranch was massive. It took them twenty minutes to drive from the front gate on the highway to the main house. Ty led the way in his car while Rio followed him in hers.

The ranch house was a sprawling one-story adobe with a red tile roof and arches all along the front. The barns, ranch buildings and corrals were set behind the house and to the east. The familiar sights and sounds made Rio homesick suddenly, but she made herself smile as Ty carried her luggage and ushered her into the cool interior of the tiled entry hall.

Ty's housekeeper was a Mexican-American woman with a wide smile and dark eyes that sparkled with good humor. She welcomed Rio effusively, then led the way to a guest room.

At supper that evening, Maria proved to be every

bit the good cook that Ty had boasted, and her happy, gracious presence as she bustled in and out from the kitchen put Rio at ease. Ty was an even better conversationalist than in the past, and his pleasant, easygoing banter lifted her spirits tremendously. Rio ate more at that meal than she had in weeks, but afterward, she became so sleepy that she could barely keep her eyes open.

Ty saw her to her room, then thanked her for accepting his invitation. He asked if she'd like to go for an early ride to see part of the ranch, and seemed pleased when she said yes.

That night, Rio got the best night's sleep she'd gotten in what felt like months. She awoke the next morning less heartsore, and realized that for the first time in a long time, she looked forward to the day.

Before she knew it, Ty had persuaded her to stay at the ranch far longer than the one night she'd meant to. She felt better staying at Cameron than anywhere she'd been these past weeks. She wasn't certain exactly why that was, other than her private speculation that ranch life was far more familiar to her than cities and traveling.

She wished she could credit a romantic attraction to Ty with her improved outlook on life. Though he'd made no secret of his interest in her, Rio could summon no more than a distant appreciation for Ty's sunburnished good looks and a pleasant feeling of friendship toward him.

It was on the fifth morning of her visit that the two of them were down at one of the corrals watching one of the wranglers put a showy two-year-old Arabian gray through her paces on a longe line. They were standing together at the fence when Ty's hand brushed hers.

As if merely touching her had given him the idea, he took her hand and threaded his fingers with hers.

Rio had to force herself not to automatically pull her hand from his. She tried to be patient as he casually rubbed his thumb across her knuckles. The tiny spark of feminine response she felt gave her hope for a mere instant before the sudden memory of Kane's bold touch doused it. Though her heart had felt numb for weeks, the sharp memory pricked it.

"You're as tense as a bronc about to blow, Rio. Are you just skittish, or does my touch put you off?" Ty had been the soul of tact and gentlemanly behavior her whole visit, but his question was to the point.

Rio was overwhelmed by a surge of emotion so strong that she couldn't speak for a moment. She gave his hand a tentative squeeze of apology, then felt his warm, hard grip tighten in silent consolation.

"I'm sorry, Ty," she said softly. She couldn't look him in the eye, she couldn't have looked anyone in the eye while she said, "Your touch doesn't put me off, but it does remind me of someone I'm trying to forget." Her voice broke unexpectedly on the last word.

"Kane Langtry?"

Ty's question had come so quickly that it made her breath catch, but she gave a stiff nod.

He chuckled. "Well, I reckon you came to the right place," he said, then leaned close. His voice went low to drawl out the shameless brag, "I'll have you know,

Rio Cory, that I'm probably one of the few men in Texas who could make you forget all about Kane Langtry...if you're sure you want to forget.''

Rio gave another stiff nod. "I have to.''

Ty released her hand and slid an arm around her shoulders to pull her against his side. "Then give it time, darlin'.''

Rio hesitated, then slid her arm around his lean middle. Neither of them said more as they watched the Arab filly.

Kane stared at the fax the private investigator had just sent. After weeks of waiting for Rio to come home to Langtry or to at least call him, he'd finally given in and hired an investigator. It galled him to have to do such a thing, but he'd done it.

He'd fumed over their broken engagement and the cavalier note she'd left for him. If she'd turned out to be the spoiled brat in her note, then to hell with her. It took all of a day for his fury to burn itself out. The rest of the time since then, he'd carried around an ache that rarely eased. He blamed himself for Rio's flight.

She had taken his father's death hard. The riding accident had to have been traumatic for her, though she'd taken her share of spills before. His sudden proposal, his insistence on a large wedding and his impatience to have it soon might have been too much.

Rio was strong, but she felt things deeply. She was a reserved woman, shy and sometimes self-conscious. Her aversion to drawing attention to herself might have made the prospect of a huge wedding frightening.

He'd concluded all this from what he thought he knew about her. He'd hired the investigator to find her so he'd have a chance to get her back. He'd been so determined to be understanding and forgiving. He'd forgo the big wedding, he'd let her have or do whatever she wanted, as long as she came home with him. He'd meant to do everything in his power to make her happy—until he'd read the last entry of her itinerary.

According to the information that was staring him in the face, Rio might just have caught up with the newer, shinier toy she'd mentioned in her damned note.

"Would you like me to fix you a drink?" Ty asked as he joined Rio in the spacious family room at the back of the huge ranch house after supper.

Rio smiled, more and more at ease with him, but secretly troubled that she couldn't summon anything more than feelings of friendship for him. Her soft, "Nothing for me, thanks," made him nod with clear approval.

"To my knowledge, my mother never touched a drop of alcohol in her life," he said as he crossed the room. "But we've got plenty of soft drinks over here," he added as he reached the liquor cabinet and got down two crystal tumblers. "You could either choose a soft drink, ice water, or I can get you some iced tea."

He glanced back at her and she smiled. "Then pick any soft drink, lots of ice."

"Comin' up," he replied, then turned away to open the small refrigerator and select one.

Rio watched him use tongs to put ice in her glass, then pour the cola. The confidence in his every move fascinated her. Kane bore the same confidence, though his was tinged with a natural arrogance that managed to be more appealing than conceited.

The shaft of pain that speared her heart made her look away from Ty. The moment she'd first caught herself comparing Ty to Kane, she'd been horrified. From then on, her mind had been flooded with scores of examples of parallels and contrasts. She could barely notice anything about Ty anymore that her mind didn't automatically compare to Kane.

The frustration she felt suddenly made her eyes sting. She'd thought her numb emotions would somehow help her get over loving Kane. She'd thought that Ty had potential to help her forget. The bitter irony was that Ty and Kane were as disturbingly alike as they were different. She could barely look at Ty now without thinking about Kane, without longing for Kane.

"Something wrong?"

Rio started at Ty's voice so close, then realized belatedly that he'd walked over to where she sat on the sofa and was holding a tumbler of cola over ice out to her. Her soft "Sorry," and her haste to take the drink covered her lapse.

Or so she thought. Ty sat down next to her so they were touching from shoulder to hip to knee as he stretched his long legs out. He gave a deep sigh, then turned his head to look at her.

"You know, the more I'm around you, the more I realize that old saying, 'Still waters run deep,' must have been written with you in mind." He smiled at her as he reached over and slipped his hand around hers. "You've loved Kane Langtry a lot of years, haven't you?"

Rio faced forward, dismayed at the question. She made a tiny move to pull her hand away from Ty's, but his grip tightened gently. "I don't mean that as a criticism or to hurt you in any way, Rio," he said softly. "I reckon I can live with the agony if I don't thrill the daylights outta you, but I would count it a misfortune if I couldn't be your friend."

The smile she heard in his voice made her turn her head and look at him. He was smiling, a rueful, sexy, masculine smile that communicated his sincerity.

"And because I'd like to be your friend," he went on, "I'm offerin' myself as someone who'll keep your confidence to the grave, should you ever need someone to talk to."

Rio glanced away and looked down at their clasped hands. She put her other hand on top of his and rubbed it fondly. Her soft, "Thanks," was muddled by the emotion clogging her throat. How she'd love to unburden herself to Ty! He was everything she could want in a man, everything she should want in a man, but the fact that he wasn't Kane Langtry was a tragedy for her.

Suddenly she'd carried the pain and the horror long enough. She heard herself make a faltering start, "I loved Kane almost from the moment Sam moved me to the main house. At first, I looked up to him as a sort of brother...''

It took a while for Rio to get the whole story out. By the time she finished, she sat with her head back against the sofa, staring into space, almost too emotionally wrung out to move.

CHAPTER ELEVEN

"PLEASE, Kane, let me go with you," Tracy pleaded. "You're still so angry with Rio—you might need someone there to be a buffer."

Tracy trailed anxiously after him as he got ready to leave the house for the airstrip. Tracy with her large eyes and delicate, aloof ways was clearly upset and more emotional than he could ever recall her being.

On the other hand, in spite of Ramona's efforts, he didn't really know his meek little stepsister. Hell, she'd barely spent any significant time on Langtry after the first six months of his father's and Ramona's marriage, and she'd been a shy, fragile fifteen-year-old then. This weeks-long visit was turning out to be the second longest time she'd ever been around.

Kane paused and gave her a steady look. "Why should you care? I thought you and Rio didn't get along." He watched as Tracy quailed beneath his harsh gaze. She looked too fragile to be a buffer for anything tougher than a carton of eggshells, and she certainly couldn't withstand the verbal brawl he meant to have with Rio.

Tracy looked desperate for a moment before she blurted, "Rio's always been misunderstood. I—I think that's what's going on now."

Kane gave her a cynical smile. "Rio's been a lot more than misunderstood. What makes you suddenly think you're an expert on someone you can barely bring yourself to speak to?''

Tracy blushed heavily, but she was surprisingly dogged on the subject. ''Please, Kane, let me go with you. I think I can help.'' She hesitantly touched his arm, but he politely moved it away.

Ramona had been throwing Tracy at him every day since Rio had gone. He hadn't appreciated his father's attempts to matchmake, but Sam's efforts were nothing compared to Ramona's absolute determination to see the two of them wed. Tracy had seemed embarrassed by her mother's machinations, but she went along with anything Ramona wanted like a trained pet. This could be another ploy engineered by Ramona, and Kane wanted no part of it.

''This is between Rio and me. There's no need for a third party, Tracy, however good their intentions are,'' he told her, then turned away to finish throwing a few things into an overnight bag.

Once he'd zipped it shut and picked it up to turn around, he noticed that Tracy had vanished. He had other things on his mind, so he didn't give her another thought.

He stopped by the office at the bunkhouse to speak to his foreman. The veterinarian arrived and delayed him for another hour. By the time he had one of the ranch hands drive him to the airstrip, his mood was darker and more volatile than ever.

The fact that he then had to deal with Tracy, who was already waiting in the plane and refused to get out, made him so surly that neither of them spoke the whole flight to Cameron Ranch.

*　　*　　*

Ty was watching a video of cattle from an upcoming cattle sale, so Rio had come down to the stables in search of something to do.

The wrangler she'd watched work the gray filly the other day had offered to let her put the young horse through her paces and Rio had been delighted to do it. She'd finished with the filly and gave her a brisk grooming. It wasn't until she turned the horse into one of the small, shaded corrals that she let herself think of the colt she'd been working with at Langtry. Barbie, as she'd named him after all, had been healing nicely before she'd left the ranch.

All it took was thinking about the young horse to make the melancholy that never seemed to leave her settle more heavily on her heart.

Oh, Kane, how are you? Do you hate me now? She couldn't silence the questions. She'd worked so hard to keep her thoughts away from Kane, but she felt as if she'd been staggering through a mine field, stepping on one trigger after another. Was she doomed to love him the rest of her days? Why couldn't she make herself stop?

Because it can't be true.

For a moment, hope swelled her heart and lifted her spirits until the stark memory of Sam's name on her birth certificate brought her crashing back to earth. Rio reached up and gripped the wood rails of the gate as she struggled to contain her roiling emotions.

Only a coward would have kept silent all those years, she thought bitterly. Only a coward would have allowed her to find that birth certificate and suffer the terrible shock that she had. The part of her heart that

was still loyal to Sam reminded her that perhaps he
had meant to tell her, but time had run out for him
before he could.

Tears of heartache and frustration made her eyes
smart, but she stubbornly blinked them back. The confused thoughts raced around and around in her head
until she was gripping the wood rail of the gate so
hard that her fingers stung. When she let go of the
rail to look for the cause of the pain, she saw the
series of splinters across her fingers. She started to
flex her hands, winced, then stopped.

"Damn it," she whispered through gritted teeth,
then swung around and stalked toward the main
house.

She heard the small airplane circle just as she got
to the house. She glanced to the west, and shaded her
eyes against the afternoon sun. Ty wasn't expecting
anyone until early tomorrow when a buyer was flying
in. Her heart thumped oddly when she saw the small
plane, but she sternly reminded herself that Kane
wasn't the only person in Texas who owned a Cesna.
There had to be dozens exactly like his.

Determined not to speculate, she rushed into
the house.

"Looks like two more, darlin'," Ty murmured as he
used the fine points of the tweezers to catch the tip
of the next splinter. Once it was out, he angled her
hand differently under the lamp he'd placed on the
corner of the desk and went after the last one. When
he finished with the delicate job, he let go of her hand
and gave a gusty sigh.

Rio inspected her fingers beneath the light while Ty opened the bottle of peroxide and pulled a handful of cotton balls out of the bag to toss into a bowl. He had rounded everything up for her to take care of the splinters herself, then had taken over. Still upset by thoughts of Kane, she'd allowed him to, selfishly hoping...

"All right, comes the hard part," he announced, then liberally poured peroxide over the cotton balls in the small stainless steel bowl.

She looked on when he held first one hand, then the other over the bowl while he swabbed the stinging antiseptic over the tiny spots where the splinters had been.

Rio couldn't help but smile when he took a deep breath and blew strongly across her fingers to soothe the sting of the peroxide. He took another breath and repeated the process, only this time, he glanced over at her face as he did so.

One moment, Rio was looking over into the bright sparkle in his eyes. The next, Ty leaned over and kissed her gently on the lips. He pulled back slightly to whisper, "A kiss to make it better," before he was kissing her again. She felt his hand come up to the back of her head to hold her for a firmer kiss.

The low drawl that intruded was almost a growl.

"Is he the newer, shiner toy?"

Startled, Rio's eyes flew open, but Ty's firm grip kept her from pulling away until he slowly ended the kiss. He drew back, his blue eyes gleaming into hers before he turned his head to look over at Kane.

"What brings you by, Kane?" he asked, the sound of his voice somehow challenging.

Rio stared over at Kane in disbelief, the very sight of his broad-shouldered, lean-hipped body sending a longing through her that was so sharp and went so deep that she could barely breathe.

"I came to see your houseguest. She and I have some unfinished business." The smile Kane gave Ty was anything but civil.

Clearly untroubled by the aggression in Kane's stance, Ty leaned back in his chair and gave Kane a measuring look. "Miz Rio's a guest in my house. And as long as she's on Cameron Ranch, her safety and her happiness are my top priorities."

Kane's expression hardened. "You think I'd hurt her?"

Ty's expression went just as hard. "She came here hurt, Langtry. I'd say she's had enough."

Distressed, Rio suddenly came to her feet. "Please—don't." Both men gave her their complete attention and it flustered her. She looked from Kane to Ty. "Maybe it's best for me to talk to him."

"You don't have to, Rio," Ty told her gently. "I'll abide by whatever you decide, and I'll see that Kane does, too."

Though Rio wasn't looking at Kane, she felt his outrage like a sudden shock wave. She gave a nervous little shake of her head and made herself look over at him. His face was like stone, and his blue eyes blazed at her. It was difficult to tell him, "I'll talk to you, but I need to get something first." Kane started to disagree, so she quickly added, "It will explain better than I can."

Kane glared at her mistrustfully, but didn't object when she started toward the door and left the room. She reached back to close the door behind her, then turned and came to a surprised halt.

"Hello, Rio." Tracy was standing in the hall, squeezing the life out of the small handbag she had in her delicate hands. "I—I've come to tell you something."

Despite her upset at Kane's sudden appearance on Cameron Ranch, Rio couldn't help but be astonished. Not only because Tracy had come, too, but because Tracy was actually speaking to her. Her cold, aloof manner had faded to a nervous, clearly miserable one.

Rio watched, a bit amazed as delicate, perfectly turned out Tracy LeDeux, who'd always been grace personified, fumbled awkwardly with her handbag, nearly managing to drop it before she got out a folded paper.

"Here," she said as she shoved the paper toward Rio. "I'm so sorry."

Rio raised her hand to take it, then saw the backside of the notary imprint on the paper and froze.

Tracy anxiously pushed it against her fingers. "Please—look at it. It's your birth certificate."

Rio pushed it back and shook her head. "No thanks. I already know."

"No, you don't," Tracy insisted, and Rio saw the definite sparkle of tears in her eyes. "Please read it." Tracy's face was anguished, and Rio's own anguish rose.

Again she shook her head and started to step around Tracy. Tracy caught her arm urgently. "S-Sam Langtry isn't your father," she blurted, then flinched as Rio abruptly turned toward her.

"The birth certificates in that book and in your mother's papers are forged," Tracy said tearfully.

Stunned, Rio stared at her a moment, then demanded, "How? The book Sam left me was locked in a drawer and no one but Sam knew about my mother's papers." Oh, God, how miraculous it would be if the birth certificates had been forged, but she couldn't let herself hope.

Tracy was losing the battle not to cry. "My mother found the book and the papers," she got out. "She'd gone into your room when no one knew and she found the letter Sam left you. That was when she found out about the book with your mother's flowers and pictures and keepsakes. S-she went through everything of yours and found your real birth certificate. Then she hired a forger—I don't know who—then found Sam's book and put one fake birth certificate there, then put the other one in with your mother's papers."

The tremor that quaked through Rio made her feel faint. She put out a hand to the wall for support.

"I'm so sorry. I should have done something, I should have said something before now. But I c-couldn't—I know my mother h-has a problem, but I hoped she'd—" Tracy's breath caught as Rio looked at her. "I'm sorry, Rio, so sorry!" Tracy suddenly broke down but she was still trying to push the birth certificate into Rio's hand.

Rio was in shock. Hopeful, yet terrified, she took

the paper and unfolded it. The forgeries were so imprinted on her mind that she could see right away that this paper had the slight off-white color of age.

"A-and here," Tracy sniffed. "I s-sent for a copy of your birth certificate. It came two days ago, but I never opened the envelope, in case you needed more proof." Tracy was pawing awkwardly through the handbag, her eyes so blurred by the tears that were spilling down her flushed cheeks that she was having a hard time seeing. She finally got the envelope and passed it to Rio.

A fresh wave of terror gripped Rio's heart. She couldn't bring herself to open the envelope and see for herself, but this was too important for her not to make certain. She hadn't let herself read the name in the father space on the other one, because she couldn't bear to see Sam Langtry's name in the space again.

"So you've known from the day Rio left."

Kane's voice was chilling. It startled both Tracy and Rio, and they turned their heads to look at him. Ty stood beside and just a bit behind Kane, his expression just as forbidding. Either man in a mood as dark would have been formidable. Both standing together, with Tracy the sole focus of their attention, was downright horrifying.

"N-not from the first day. Not until a few days later, but I've known for a long time," Tracy admitted shakily. "I was hoping Rio was going to that county to check the birth records herself. W-when she didn't come back, then I knew I had to do something right away." Tracy sucked in a huge sob, then choked on it a bit. "But I couldn't," she got out.

"You left because of a forged birth certificate?" Kane asked grimly.

Rio nodded. "I'll get them." On legs that shook so badly she could barely walk straight, she rushed toward the guest wing of the sprawling home. Once there, she found what she was after in seconds, then hurried back to the den.

The other three had gone into the den and Rio hesitated in the doorway before she walked toward Kane and handed him the birth certificates Tracy said were forged. Kane took them quickly, then glanced at them a moment before he stepped over to the lamp that was still sitting on the corner of Ty's big desk.

"The one with Ned Cory's name has little correction tape marks beneath it. If you hold it closer to the light, you can see that they spell out Sam's name," she told him, then gripped the envelope and the folded document Tracy had given her.

When she couldn't bear the suspense another second, she made herself unfold the paper. Ned Cory's name was clearly printed exactly where it should have been. Rio walked over to the lamp and used the bright light to inspect it closer.

Relief unlike any she'd ever felt started deep in her heart and spread in slow, repeated waves through her mind, body and emotions until she felt limp with calm. It didn't trouble her now to slip a finger beneath the flap of the envelope and tear it open. The duplicate birth certificate inside also bore Ned Cory's name.

Kane's voice was low. "I could have told you we weren't related, Rio. My father wouldn't have had so many romantic plans for us, and he never would have left me a letter that told me how much a fool I'd be if I let some other lucky bastard marry you.''

Rio looked up into the dark fire in his eyes. ''He never said anything to me. In my letter, he called me his precious daughter. So, when I found the birth certificate in the book he'd left for me that had been locked up in a drawer you had trouble finding a key for—'' She had to stop and look down. She bit her lip a moment while she waited for the surge of emotion to ease.

''I wanted you to hate me,'' she whispered, then looked up at him. ''I didn't want you to know you were planning to marry your own half-sister.'' She offered him a faint smile that trembled precariously.

''So does this mean...'' Kane let his voice trail off. The vulnerability she saw in him just then shook her. Kane had never in his life been vulnerable. ''I love you, Rio. Please come home.''

Rio's soft ''I love you,'' was the catalyst.

Kane suddenly took the step that separated them and caught her up, crushing her against himself as he buried his face in her hair. Her feet no longer on the floor, Rio wrapped her arms around his neck and dropped the documents as she held on to him and cried.

Moments later, he was kissing her, hard, desperate, hungry kisses that made her wild with passion. Neither of them knew it when Ty took Tracy's arm and quietly escorted her from the room.

''Never leave me, never leave me,'' Kane chanted gruffly when they paused to catch their breaths. ''Oh, baby, anything you ever want, anything you ever want me to do, it's yours. As long as there's breath in my body, I'll get it for you, I'll do it for you, only don't leave me again."

Rio flexed the fingers she'd combed into his thick black hair, ignoring the slight sting as she angled his head so she could kiss him again. The edge of pain in his low voice compelled her to reassure him, but she was too overwhelmed to speak. She couldn't get enough of the feel and taste and male strength of him. She'd been starving…

The warm breeze blew lightly at the Painted Fence, riffling their shirts and toying with Rio's hip-length hair until it danced in the air around her like a sable aura.

Kane watched as she bent down and tenderly placed half of the red sweetheart roses in the bronze vase on her mother's grave. She straightened, then walked around the headstone to the vase on his father's grave and placed the rest of the small, perfect roses there.

When she finished, she straightened again, then glanced his way and smiled a soft, sad smile. He held out his hand, and she walked toward him, bypassing his hand to instead step into his arms to hug him and press her cheek against his chest.

"I love you more than my life, Rio Langtry," he whispered as he tightened his arms around her. His voice was rough with the emotion that still surprised him with its fervency.

"I love you more than mine," she whispered back as she rubbed her cheek against the soft cotton of his shirtfront and snuggled closer.

"Are you feeling all right?" he asked gently, then drew back and slid a finger under her chin to coax her to look at him. Rio complied and smiled up at him, the light sheen of sentimental tears clearing slowly from her beautiful blue eyes.

"Never better. Pregnancy must agree with me. So far, at least," she added, then reached behind her for his hand and brought it around to press it against the slight swell of her belly.

Kane's face went stern. "I still think you ought to stay off horses and stop working with the men."

"I will soon," she told him, then pulled his hand from between them so she could hug him tighter.

She heard the frown in his voice when he grumbled, "That's what you said a week ago. How soon is soon?"

"Soon," she said as if soon was a definite date on the calendar.

As much as she'd loved Kane, as long as she'd loved him, she'd never suspected how wonderful it would be to be loved by him and to love him openly, fully, with all her heart. In the year since their wedding, love had been a revelation for them both. Kane's love and devotion had steadied her, given her confidence and soothed old wounds. Her love for him had gentled him and made him tenderhearted, though he was just as stern and fierce a man as he'd ever been.

"Don't wait too long," he said gruffly. "My nerves are raggedy enough."

Rio laughed and drew back. "You haven't had a nervous minute in your life."

"Not until lately," he groused, but she could see

the faint twitch that told her he was trying not to smile.

"I love you, Rio. Somehow I can never say it to you often enough." He brought a hand up to her cheek.

Rio smiled, then pulled her arms from around his lean middle and went up on tiptoe to wrap her arms around his neck.

"Go ahead and say it as often as you like. I'm never going to get tired of hearing it." She pulled his head down to hers and kissed him, deeply, passionately.

Kane suddenly loosened his hold to bend and catch her behind the knees to lift her in his arms. He ended the kiss and pressed his forehead against hers. A rare, boyish smile came over his lips.

"When I was getting the roses for them, I got a couple of armloads for you, Mrs. Langtry. The problem is, every one of them is up in our room. Now the whole bedroom smells like that bath oil you use sometimes when you think you've got to do something extra to get my attention." He paused to place a brief, tender kiss on her lips. "I don't think I can wait till tonight to...show 'em to you."

Rio smiled. "I don't think I can wait until tonight to...see them," she said softly, then held on tight as Kane turned and strode toward the pickup that was parked just outside the gate.

✦. _Harlequin Romance®_

is pleased to offer

Authors you'll treasure,
books you'll want to keep!

These are romances we know you'll love reading—
over and over again! Because they are,
quite simply, the best....

Watch for these special books by some of your
favorite authors:

#3468 WILD AT HEART
by Susan Fox (August 1997)

#3471 DO YOU TAKE THIS COWBOY?
by Jeanne Allan (September 1997)

#3477 NO WIFE REQUIRED!
by Rebecca Winters (October 1997)

Available in August, September and October 1997
wherever Harlequin books are sold.

Let's Celebrate!

invites you to
the party of the season!

Grab your popcorn and be prepared to laugh as we celebrate with **LOVE & LAUGHTER**.

Harlequin's newest series is going Hollywood!

Let us make you laugh with three months of terrific books, authors and romance, plus a chance to win a FREE 15-copy video collection of the best romantic comedies ever made.

For more details look in the back pages of any Love & Laughter title, from July to September, at your favorite retail outlet.

Don't forget the popcorn!

Available wherever
Harlequin books are sold.

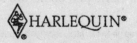
HARLEQUIN®

Don't miss these Harlequin favorites by some of our most popular authors! And now you can receive a discount by ordering two or more titles!

HT#25700	HOLDING OUT FOR A HERO by Vicki Lewis Thompson	$3.50 U.S. ☐/$3.99 CAN.☐
HT#25699	WICKED WAYS by Kate Hoffmann	$3.50 U.S. ☐/$3.99 CAN.☐
HP#11845	RELATIVE SINS by Anne Mather	$3.50 U.S. ☐/$3.99 CAN.☐
HP#11849	A KISS TO REMEMBER by Miranda Lee	$3.50 U.S. ☐/$3.99 CAN.☐
HR#03359	FAITH, HOPE AND MARRIAGE by Emma Goldrick	$2.99 U.S. ☐/$3.50 CAN.☐
HR#03433	TEMPORARY HUSBAND by Day Leclaire	$3.25 U.S. ☐/$3.75 CAN.☐
HS#70679	QUEEN OF THE DIXIE DRIVE-IN by Peg Sutherland	$3.99 U.S. ☐/$4.50 CAN.☐
HS#70712	SUGAR BABY by Karen Young	$3.99 U.S. ☐/$4.50 CAN.☐
HI#22319	BREATHLESS by Carly Bishop	$3.50 U.S. ☐/$3.99 CAN.☐
HI#22335	BEAUTY VS. THE BEAST by M.J. Rodgers	$3.50 U.S. ☐/$3.99 CAN.☐
AR#16577	BRIDE OF THE BADLANDS by Jule McBride	$3.50 U.S. ☐/$3.99 CAN.☐
AR#16656	RED-HOT RANCHMAN by Victoria Pade	$3.75 U.S. ☐/$4.25 CAN.☐
HH#28868	THE SAXON by Margaret Moore	$4.50 U.S. ☐/$4.99 CAN.☐
HH#28893	UNICORN VENGEANCE by Claire Delacroix	$4.50 U.S. ☐/$4.99 CAN.☐

(limited quantities available on certain titles)

	TOTAL AMOUNT	$ _____
DEDUCT:	10% DISCOUNT FOR 2+ BOOKS	$ _____
	POSTAGE & HANDLING	$ _____
	($1.00 for one book, 50¢ for each additional)	
	APPLICABLE TAXES*	$ _____
	TOTAL PAYABLE	$ _____
	(check or money order—please do not send cash)	

To order, complete this form, along with a check or money order for the total above, payable to Harlequin Books, to: **In the U.S.**: 3010 Walden Avenue, P.O. Box 9047, Buffalo, NY 14269-9047; **In Canada**: P.O. Box 613, Fort Erie, Ontario, L2A 5X3.

Name: _____

Address: _____ City: _____

State/Prov.: _____ Zip/Postal Code: _____

*New York residents remit applicable sales taxes.
Canadian residents remit applicable GST and provincial taxes.

Look us up on-line at: http://www.romance.net   HBKJS97

Reach new heights of passion and adventure this August in

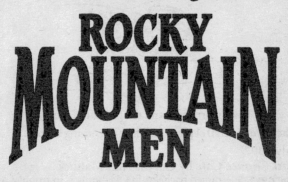

ROCKY MOUNTAIN MEN

Don't miss this exciting new collection featuring three stories of Rocky Mountain men and the women who dared to tame them.

CODE OF SILENCE
by Linda Randall Wisdom

SILVER LADY
by Lynn Erickson

TOUCH THE SKY
by Debbi Bedford

Available this August wherever
Harlequin and Silhouette books are sold.

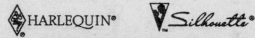

**HARLEQUIN AND SILHOUETTE
ARE PLEASED TO PRESENT**

Love, marriage—and the pursuit of family!

Check your retail shelves for these upcoming titles:

July 1997
Last Chance Cafe by Curtiss Ann Matlock
The most determined bachelor in Oklahoma is in trouble! A
lovely widow with three daughters has moved next door—and
the girls want a dad! But he wants to know if their mom needs
a husband....

August 1997
Thorne's Wife by Joan Hohl
Pennsylvania. It was only to be a marriage of convenience—
until they fell in love! Now, three years later, tragedy
threatens to separate them forever and Valerie wants only to
be in the strength of her husband's arms. For she has some
very special news for the expectant father...

September 1997
Desperate Measures by Paula Detmer Riggs
New Mexico judge Amanda Wainwright's daughter has been
kidnapped, and the price of her freedom is a verdict in
favor of a notorious crime boss. So enters ex-FBI agent
Devlin Buchanan—ruthless, unstoppable—and soon there is
no risk he will not take for her.

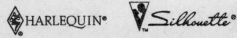

HARLEQUIN®   Silhouette®